Fiona smiled and felt color rising in her face. She wanted to nestle her face in those lovely breasts and suckle their warmth, but she knew better. Louise couldn't be ravished into making love. She had to be coaxed, gently. Sex was something a little too raw for Louise's refined nature. This didn't help Fiona's attitude of wanting to thump her bones, of wanting to take her roughly, ardently, to take her places she'd never let herself go, to take her over the edge to total abandon, to make her want and want so bad she'd let go and let Fiona break through, to feel her, know her, touch her.

Louise smiled back. Fiona felt herself grow warm, wondering if once again she would be disappointed, the endless teenage-boy syndrome always hoping this time she'd get laid. Would tonight be the night she'd get lucky?

LOOKING FOR NAIAD?

Buy our books at
www.naiadpress.com

or call our toll-free number
1-800-533-1973

or by fax (24 hours a day)
1-850-539-9731

BOTH SIDES

BY
SAXON BENNETT

THE NAIAD PRESS, INC.
1999

Printed in the United States of America on acid-free paper
First Edition

Editor: Lila Empson
Cover designer: Bonnie Liss (Phoenix Graphics)
Typesetter: Sandi Stancil

Library of Congress Cataloging-in-Publication Data

Bennett, Saxon, 1961 –
    Both sides / by Saxon Bennett.
        p.   cm.
    ISBN 1-56280-236-4   (alk. paper)
    I. Title.
PS3552.E547544B68   1999
813'.54—dc21   98-46300
                                                                      CIP

To Lin and Boy-Boy
with much love for teaching me
how to hokeypokey in the sixth dimension.
Life would be very dull without you.

Acknowledgments

Many thanks to Richard Terry for his expertise in the field of computers. He has saved more than one novel from the clutches of my computer errors. As well as being an honorary lesbian, he is my number one fan.

About the Author

Saxon Bennett lives in Phoenix, Arizona, with her lovely partner and furry pet pal. She is still learning a lot about her favorite subject which, of course, would be lesbians and wishes someday that we might have our own planet when the human races move about in the universe. Until then, she is content with her family and friends and hopes to hold many a picnic in nirvana.

Books by Saxon Bennett

The Wish List
Old Ties
A Question of Love
Both Sides

One

In a yellow streak of a Volkswagen, they screamed past the lush landscape of early summer. But Jane believed in speeding. A speed limit was a barrier set forth to impede personal progress. No one was going to tell her how fast she could drive. Jane Graves was an anarchist of the fiercest order. She flew wherever she went. Seat belts were optional. Adrienne gritted her teeth and held on for dear life. Jane's girlfriend, Claudette Benet, chatted amiably, immune to the fact they were going ninety up a twisting narrow road on a Friday afternoon in upstate Minnesota, the busiest time of the day, year, century.

"Did I tell you I suffer from car sickness?" Adrienne said, groaning and leaning her head against the window.

Jane handed her a crumpled McDonald's bag from under the front seat. "Here, use this."

"You're so helpful," Adrienne replied.

"I try," Jane said, winking at her in the rearview mirror.

Claudette turned around, "Wait until you get a load of Jane's sister. If you think Jane is darling, Fiona is absolutely stunning, and so is her girlfriend, Louise. We call them the dynamic duo."

"Why? Because they dress up and play Batman and Robin?" Adrienne asked.

"No, silly, because they have money, good looks, drive and intelligence. Every lesbian's dream," Claudette said.

"Why do you say that?" Adrienne asked.

"Say what?" Claudette said, looking puzzled.

"Every lesbian's dream," Adrienne asked.

"Because who wouldn't want someone who is smart, good looking, driven, and rich?" Claudette said.

"There must be a fatal flaw somewhere. No one is that perfect," Adrienne said.

"I don't know, Adrienne, the dynamic duo is right up there," Jane said, smiling at her in the rearview mirror.

Adrienne smiled back.

"I got you into lots of trouble, didn't I?" Jane said.

"No, I got me into lots of trouble."

"You didn't have to tell her," Claudette said.

Adrienne blanched.

"You look surprised. Jane told me. I knew anyway. I knew the moment you two met that you'd end up sleeping together," Claudette replied matter-of-factly.

"How could you possibly know that?"

"There's a certain energy or chemistry between two people that's undeniable. Those people are then destined to become lovers," Claudette explained.

"It doesn't bother you?" Adrienne asked, running her fingers through her short hair and looking extremely nervous.

"Why should it bother me?"

"I slept with your wife."

"She's not my wife. She's my best friend, my companion, a patriot in arms in the fight against the patriarchy, but she is nothing so banal as my wife. The word *wife* implies ownership. I don't own her, which is why we've gotten along so well for so long."

"Four years is a long time," Adrienne conceded. She and Julia had only lasted two. And the last year had been absolute hell.

Adrienne and Julia had barely beenkeeping the relationship going before Adrienne left for the summer to do an internship with the Dyke Defenders, last summer when Adrienne slept with Jane. She came back a changed woman, not so much from sleeping with Jane, she told herself, although that was a definite factor, but rather from her change in politics.

All points of reference had been turned inside out and backward until she couldn't stop seeing the world as a distinct dichotomy of us *vs.* them. She remembered the night Jane made her repeat after her *us, them, us, them*. Until you understand that, you're

3

bowed under their yoke and utterly brainwashed. There's us and there's them. You've got to choose a side. Which side will it be?

Adrienne made her choice and proceeded through the gauntlet of growing pains that becoming an activist requires. She fought with everyone on the *them* side, including Julia. It had not been a good year. Her confession was the final straw.

Julia had not been happy about Adrienne's newly acquired duties of setting up a chapter of Dyke Defenders. Julia had accused Adrienne of spending more time with her *sister* Jane than with her.

"Is there something I should know about you two?" Julia had asked.

"Besides our name, address, and social security number," Adrienne replied flippantly.

"Dammit, Adrienne, can't you answer a simple question?"

"Ask one."

"Are you sleeping with her?" Julia asked.

"Would it make a difference?"

"Of course it would," Julia said, hurt in her eyes.

"She's involved with someone," Adrienne replied.

"That doesn't answer my question. Did you sleep with her?"

Adrienne felt cornered. Should she lie?

Adrienne remembered Jane looking at her askance that rainy afternoon and asking if she'd ever been attracted to someone and stepped outside the boundaries of monogamy to touch, feel, and know this other person. Adrienne had looked at her, confused.

"What do you mean?"

"I mean, haven't you ever wanted someone and just went with it, fuck the consequences?" Jane asked.

"Jane, you know I'm much too organized for that."

"I'm going to make you unorganized," Jane said, leaning over and kissing her.

Adrienne didn't back away. She let Jane kiss her, straddle her hips, take off her shirt, suck her nipples, work her way down her stomach, and take her in her mouth. She propped herself up while Jane took her from behind, filling orifices, listening while Jane told her she knew Adrienne would be wild. And she was.

Jane ended up covered in black smudges from all the pasteups they'd been photocopying, using a machine expropriated from an insurance office. They promised Natalie they'd have it smuggled back in the morning. They made copies and love all night, fulfilling everyone's promises. In the morning they got the copy machine back and went out for breakfast at a sleazy uptown diner. Adrienne had never felt more alive.

That afternoon Adrienne asked Jane if Claudette didn't wonder where she'd been spending her time.

"She knows I'm making love to you."

"What!"

"You heard me. Now come here. I'm not done with you," Jane said, grabbing her and pinning her arms to the bed like Jesus on the cross.

Religious images passed through Adrienne's head, confessions full of lust, greed, and adultery.

"I'm committing adultery, and so are you," Adrienne told her.

"Only if you subscribe to the doctrine. Making love

is beautiful, nothing more, nothing less. Culture makes it crass. Culture mandates where, when, and how. It's just like English class; you forget everything you know when you learn to write poetry."

"Jane . . ."

"Did you?" Julia asked again.

Adrienne's face gave it away.

"You did. How could I be so stupid? I should have known. Are you still fucking her?"

"No, it's not like that," Adrienne said. She remembered having felt relief when Jane had told her she wouldn't want her as a girlfriend, that casual was best. You give your best, you take only the best. Friends can fuck and still be friends, Jane had explained. It's an extension of friendship, a beautiful expression that women are capable of when they live outside the rules of patriarchy.

At the time, that was exactly how Adrienne had felt. But somehow Jane's rhetoric wasn't going to help her now. She knew she'd have to leave Julia. If she could cheat so easily, her bond with Julia was not strong enough to keep her close for much longer.

"What is it like then?" Julia said, her face flushed with anger.

"I can't explain it," Adrienne lamely replied.

"You can think of an answer while you pack," Julia said as she stormed out the room.

Adrienne packed. Jane came and picked her up, and now they were flying across the cow-dotted land-scape.

Her summer vacation had begun, and now she was

6

looking at Claudette and feeling bad — bad for her, bad for Julia, bad for herself for being such a shitheel, a homewrecker — and feeling like one of those men that make a woman love them and then move on to break other hearts.

Jane said, "Adrienne, stop looking so glum. You're being ridiculous. You know our being lovers was simply a catalyst for other things. Your relationship with Julia was already long over. You knew it and so did she. Sometimes it takes someone else to give that ever-so-gentle shove."

Claudette said, "You can't spend your life prostrate to an ideal. You loved Julia once, but you only get one life, so far as we know. Do you want to spend it with a woman you no longer love? Kneeling to the goddess of lesbian longevity will not make you an angel; true love will."

"But I thought it was true love," Adrienne replied.

"Was it ever painful?" Claudette inquired.

"What do you mean?"

"Did you think you were going to die if you didn't see her? Did you feel her coursing through your veins, filling your insides, crowding your thoughts, holding your soul gently in her hands? Or did you think, We talk, we don't fight, I need a roommate, I'm tired of being alone, and the sex is good? Were you thinking or lusting? Were you scrambling the heights or were you settling?" Claudette said.

"You have the most poetic mind," Jane said, admiration shining in her eyes.

"Well?" Claudette said.

"I don't know. Ask me in a month."

"Why a month?" Claudette asked.

"It's an arbitrary unit of time."

"Lame," Jane said, meeting Adrienne's gaze in the rearview mirror. "This weekend will take your mind off it."

"*Her*. Take my mind off *her*."

"This is not about Julia. It's how you feel about *you*. She's not the one for you. Don't waste your time. True love walks in the door and, bam, you'll never think of her again, guaranteed," Jane said.

"If I remember correctly, your last guarantee got us both thrown in jail, and it wasn't on a Monopoly board, either."

"No small task. In downtown's toughest precinct with the hookers. I remember. Some of which, I might add, joined up later, organizing against their pimps. An evening well spent."

"All right, there were moments," Adrienne conceded.

"Do you remember what I told you when they were throwing us in the paddy wagon?" Jane asked.

"You said that a person can be scared for a few minutes or for all her life. And you asked me which I preferred," Adrienne said.

"Which have you been abiding by?"

"I'm oscillating between them."

Jane frowned at her in the mirror.

"Jane, watch out!" Adrienne said.

It was too late, the bunny rabbit went thud beneath the tires.

"Damn!" Jane said.

"See, Adrienne, that was an oscillating bunny and look what happened. Sit in the middle of the road too long and a Janemobile will flatten you," Claudette said.

"At least it was quick. That's an act of kindness," Jane said.

Adrienne groaned. Craziness, pure and simple.

Louise was making dinner when they arrived. The formal dining room was set in tasteful elegance, and Jane was required to wear a shirt. Jane preferred sports bras or skimpy tank tops to any other attire. If she could get away with going topless, she would. She hoped, as she did every summer, to convince the group to challenge the law that made it mandatory for women to cover their breasts. Jane did have lovely breasts. Out of respect to Louise, however, she would wear her dinner shirt, the one they kept for her in the hall closet.

Adrienne sipped a glass of merlot while Louise filled Jane in on the family happenings. Claudette was right. Louise was a very pretty woman. She had that classic sort of elegance, a Grecian profile, high cheekbones and sharp blue eyes accented by a stylish, short hairdo, probably one of those seventy-five-dollar cuts at a tasteful salon, Adrienne thought. And as straight people would say, she didn't look like a lesbian, based on the premise that she was pretty, wore makeup, and was well coiffed. She was a no-nonsense career woman, a computer programmer independently contracted. Adrienne envisioned Louise smartly attired in a dark blue blazer with an insignia on the breast pocket at one of those snobby career women clubs, cruising the crowd and making new contacts and sustaining old bonds for the purpose of improving her business acumen.

Adrienne was trying with great difficulty not to be amused by Jane's methodology as she engaged in verbal repartee with Louise, who was covering her irritation by graciously sidestepping the uncomfortable issues Jane insisted on bringing up. At the moment it was easy because she was cooking. Adrienne got the idea that being good at things was important in this house.

"So where is she?" Jane asked, finally tiring of trying to upset Louise.

"Fiona?"

"Who else?"

"Out running, shedding the week's problems and coming back cleansed," Louise answered, looking at her watch. "And depending on how far she runs this week, she should be back just about now."

"You time her?" Jane asked.

"You can almost set your watch by her, seven-and-a-half-minute miles, on average."

There was a thud, thud, coming up the driveway and then someone walking around in circles. Adrienne could see a dark-haired woman stretching and cooling down. A tall woman with never-ending legs. When Fiona strode into the kitchen she was Artemis recreated in modern form, complete with expensive running shoes. Adrienne blushed when Jane introduced her. Fiona met her gaze and smiled graciously.

Fiona took the proffered towel from Louise, wiping her face and bare midriff. Stomach muscles to die for, Adrienne thought, trying her best not to look. Claudette was right. Fiona was absolutely beautiful.

"Jane, I see you've been killing off the wildlife again. Someone is going to report you to the Fish and Game Department if you don't stop annihilating our natural resources," Fiona chided.

"How did you know?" Jane asked.

"Your tires are full of fur and other various animal parts."

"Damn! I hate when that happens," Jane said.

"It wouldn't happen if you stopped running over the poor creatures. What was it this time? A rabbit?"

"Good guess. Yep. Little Mister Bunny didn't run fast enough."

"One rabbit is better than fifty birds. Maybe you're improving inadvertently. That one was a real mess, and on my car, I might add."

"I cleaned it up," Jane declared, looking slightly offended.

"True, but initially the car looked like you drove it through a slaughterhouse. I believe you greatly affected the sparrow population that year," Fiona teased.

"It was nasty," Jane admitted. "I remember looking in the rearview mirror and seeing the road covered in flattened birds. It was disgusting. It was a good thing Claudette wasn't with me. She would have puked at the sight of that much flesh. But I thought the birds would move. They usually do."

"*Usually* being the operative word here. They probably saw you coming, made ready for flight, and died before they knew what hit them," Fiona said.

"Birds are quick, but Jane is quicker," Claudette said, giving her a gentle shove.

"Don't start," Jane said.

"Dinner smells wonderful, darling," Fiona said, putting her arm around Louise's waist.

"I hope so. This is something new, and I'm rather concerned."

"She's an incredible cook," Fiona told Adrienne, who nodded shyly.

"I'd better go shower," Fiona said.

"I'll say," Louise said, pushing her away.

"Please, no additional commentary from the gallery. We are already aware of our vices," Fiona said, heading off.

"Adrienne, come help me hose off the car. Claudette is squeamish when it comes to animal products. Fucking vegetarians," Jane said.

"Watch it!" Adrienne retorted.

"I know. It's no wonder you and Claudette get along so well, my herbaceous beauties," Jane said, tousling what short locks they both had left after the last shaving debacle. Adrienne and Claudette pulled away like embarrassed teenagers.

Louise raised an eyebrow. She had often entertained the notion that Jane and Claudette's relationship was not strictly monogamous. She was glad that Fiona was far more stable than her sister. Louise often wondered at what level, if any, a sense of decorum began in Jane's twisted mind. But Jane was Fiona's sister. She loved Fiona. She would love her sister too. Love required obligation. Louise was good at obligation. She'd built a life on it. She thought of life as a swift-running, particularly treacherous and unruly river that required many sturdy bridges to allow for passage. Social obligation was one of those bridges.

While Jane and Adrienne washed the car, Claudette asked Louise culinary questions. Louise was skeptical about Claudette's sincerity in her interests. She suspected that Claudette was simply making conversation and murmuring appropriate responses. She was so damned amiable it was difficult to tell.

Jane grabbed Adrienne's hand once they were outside and away from peering eyes. Louise would never understand this one. They went around back and got the hose. Jane pulled Adrienne close.

"I've missed you. Are you all right?"

"I'm okay," Adrienne said, avoiding Jane's gaze.

Jane took Adrienne's face in her hands, making her look at her.

"No, you're not. You're hurting. I never wanted to hurt you."

"It's not you. I could have lied when Julia asked, but I didn't want to. What happened between us happened for a reason."

"You're not just saying that to appease my guilty conscience?" Jane asked.

"You're completely amoral. *Guilt* is not in your repertoire of behavioral ills."

"I haven't completely eradicated guilt from my psyche. One cannot escape the puritanical so easily."

Jane kissed her gently.

They dragged the hose out and sprayed off the car. Getting the fur out of the tires proved more difficult. Adrienne made Jane do it.

"Let me guess. Principles?"

"You got it. Herbivores don't do fur," Adrienne said.

Adrienne sprayed while Jane dug stuff out of the tires.

"If I truly subscribed to the proletariat doctrine, I would have bald tires and this wouldn't be a problem."

"What do good tires have to do with politics?"

"They're bourgeois," Jane said.

"No, they're not. A fur coat, a Rolex watch, or a Mercedes-Benz would be against your politics. You have a piece of shit for a car, you live in a pit, and you put all your money into the Dyke Defenders. You needed these, and your father worried about you driving around on bald tires. I can't imagine why, considering you drive like a bat out of hell."

"I know. They were my last true act of acquiescence for the sake of love. I allowed him to buy me new tires because I loved him. Damn, I miss him. He was so smart, so with it, and then so sick. I remember his tired-looking eyes and his smile. He didn't have enough in him to make them sparkle like they used to."

"I'm sorry," Adrienne said, putting her arms around Jane.

"I know. I'm okay, really," Jane said, taking a deep breath.

"Okay," Adrienne said, getting up.

Jane was hurting, still bristling from the pain of losing him. She could be flippant about most things. Her father was not one of them.

She switched gears quickly. Putting those thoughts behind her, she went back to work. Who would have thought one stupid rabbit could make such a mess?

Adrienne was watching the pigeons scrambling up

on the power line and accidentally sprayed Jane with the hose.

"Hey!" Jane said, smiling with mock indignation.

"Like it hurt you," Adrienne retorted.

"Let's see how you like it," Jane said, attempting to grab the hose. Adrienne held on fast.

"No way," Adrienne said.

"Oh yeah? Let's just see."

They both ended up getting wet and wrestling on the lawn, laughing and struggling. They lay holding each other, the hose between them.

Louise and Claudette heard the ruckus and peered out the kitchen window. Claudette smiled appreciatively. Anyone that made Jane happy was nothing less than wonderful. Jane was a handful, and sometimes Claudette needed a break.

"Doesn't that bother you?" Louise asked, obviously perturbed.

"What?" Claudette asked, innocence written across her face.

"Jane out there, rolling around with another woman."

"No. Should it?" Claudette inquired.

"Well, yes. Do you two have some kind of *arrangement*?"

"Arrangement?"

"You know. You do your thing and she does hers," Louise said.

"Thing?"

Exasperated, Louise stepped outside her usual impeccable decorum, which was exactly what Claudette was aiming for. "Do you two *fuck* other people?"

"Oh that! Jane and Adrienne have slept together. And yes, I do occasionally take another lover. However, Jane is still the love of my life. Occasional tumbles are diversions that help stave off the tedium that being together too long creates."

Louise looked at her suspiciously. Was she referring to her relationship with Fiona as fourteen years of tedium? Louise wondered if beneath Claudette's amiable exterior existed the worst kind of Machiavellian.

"I see. It must be a French thing."

"Could be," Claudette responded, helping herself to another beer.

She didn't know if it was a French thing. Granted, her mother was a French Canadian, and she had grown up with her mother clamoring French invectives against her father when he attempted to regulate his wife's behavior. She was still as wild as the day he met her. Age mellowed nothing. If anything, it increased her desire for bedroom adventures. Her mother took lovers as she pleased. Her father would find out and begin his raging. Her mother would tell him to throw her out. But he never would. He'd just rage and throw things, and her mother would rage and throw things back. And then life would quiet down until the next lover came along.

Claudette had experienced firsthand what holding someone too closely could do. She and Jane understood each other. She didn't want to be restrained any more than Jane did. If it meant not being together at some point, that was preferable to making someone stay when she sought escape. They'd both seen enough of that in their friends.

Fiona finished cleaning up. She too had heard the

commotion outside. Toweling her hair dry, she went to the window and watched Jane and Adrienne wrestling on the front lawn. For a moment she was puzzled, but then she thought it best to let it alone. Jane was still young and, god knows, she was wild. Her impetuous younger sister. She loved Jane's wildness, her wildness without apology, without regret. Nothing could dampen her spirit. One condescending look from Louise, and Fiona was immediately prostrate. Fiona watched Jane laugh and thoroughly drench Adrienne with the hose. Adrienne was laughing and trying to fend her off.

Adrienne was a pretty girl, Fiona thought, despite the hairdo. Fiona didn't understand the Defenders' ritual of cutting hair in a smorgasbord of odd styles. There were dreadlocks, mohawks, completely shaved heads, and dye jobs of every conceivable hue. And some of the women had a little of everything. It was always an adventure walking downtown with them. Fiona suffered bouts of nervous tension at the mere thought of it. They looked like a pack of freaks. Fiona studied Adrienne's hair and decided a flattop was not extreme except on a woman.

Jane had tried to explain the politics of hair to Fiona. The Defenders used their bodies as a tool of protest against the glamorization of the American female. Despite Jane's efforts, Fiona wasn't convinced this kind of behavior helped the cause of lesbian civil rights. Rather, their public image appeared to play into the hands of the media by being the kind of reactionary appearance that gave ammunition to the religious right. Dyke Defenders was not quintessential lesbianism, but the media made it look that way.

Fiona tried to make Jane understand that the Defenders' sincere desire to make the world a better

17

place through their version of political action might in reality bring the movement to its knees. Jane called her a coward and walked off to perform yet another outrageous act against American culture. It would always be a point of contention between them, but sibling rivalry was nothing new. They'd been doing it most of their lives.

They hadn't gotten close until Fiona came out. Faced with an outside enemy, their rivalry seemed petty. Now they were oppressed women loving women. Fiona felt a certain angst for her parents, having the only two children in the family be gay. But what were they to do? One couldn't ask the other to give it up, to do the family right, to marry, have kids, and produce the much-wanted grandchildren.

Fiona knew it broke her mother's heart. Her mother never said anything, but Fiona could see that look in her eyes. Why? Why couldn't you? You're so lovely. They would be such darling children. Fiona would feel a pang knowing it hurt her mother, but she was unable to deny her nature. She was gay, and no amount of guilt or family obligation could change that.

Her father proved more difficult, but Jane won him over and even got him involved in the politics. He was an avid woodworker, and Jane put him to good use. He helped her with signs and banners.

Jane had been the first to tell him, the first to bring girlfriends home. Fiona didn't have the guts. She never did tell him. She had lived with Louise for years, but she didn't say and he didn't ask. But he talked to Jane about all the things that concerned him. Was it nature or nurture? What did it all mean? Where had it come from? He'd read everything he could find.

Their mother accused him of wanting to be a lesbian, so Jane made him an honorary lesbian. Fiona remembered how they'd laughed when Jane presented him with the plaque to add to his wall of plaques. He was proudest of that plaque because his favorite daughter had made it with her own hands. And they all knew Jane was not mechanically inclined. It was a miracle she hadn't cut off her hand in the process. Fiona had supervised closely.

And still Fiona couldn't form the words, couldn't say *I am*. Then it was too late, too long past. Then it would have been an insult. She hadn't hidden her life with Louise. Louise always came for the holidays, and he treated her like an in-law. But it was like the one last secret she couldn't give up, couldn't let go.

The day he died Fiona had stood in the driveway of the house studying the three small handprints cast in cement. One large and two small ones. She remembered the Sunday afternoon they had watched the cement truck dumping the driveway and the workers smoothing it to perfection. Her father had smiled mischievously, taking his small daughters to the edge of the wet cement and sticking their hands in it, marking the moment forever. If only things stayed so simple.

Then Fiona remembered Jane at the hospital draped over her father's dead body, his robust frame reduced to that of a frail old man. Jane took his death harder. He was her rock, the measure of herself, her mentor, and he was gone. She loved him deeply, loved his fight and his vigor. Jane was a lot like him, which was why they clashed so often and loved each other so fiercely.

Fiona had willingly given Jane their father's

library, and Jane packed the books about to wherever her current digs might be. Louise had suggested that Fiona store them until Jane settled down. Jane responded by saying this was as settled as she got. The books stayed with her. Her father was never farther than the first box of books. Her friends willingly carted them from place to place because they knew how much Jane loved him.

Jane had read her way through most of the collection. She was more a product of her father's library than of the expensive private school and university her father insisted they both attend.

You'll need wit and intelligence. When all else fails these things will get you through, he had told them that day in his library. Fiona could still see him standing there counseling them both. I don't care what you do for a living, he had said, but I won't have you wasting your precious brains. He had made them solemnly swear they would put forth their best efforts while away at school. He left the rest of life up to them. They both kept their promise to him. The look on his face at graduation was worth every moment of scholastic exasperation.

Now seeing Jane rolling about and playing on the front lawn made Fiona smile. She'd been worried about her younger sister. Maybe Jane was getting over their father's death.

Louise made them strip in the foyer and then go shower off the mud and grass.

"Jane, I won't have you tracking mud through this house. Now go clean up."

Adrienne noticed that she was graciously excluded from the reprimand.

Claudette made faces behind Louise's back as she

scolded. Fiona caught her in the act but only smiled. Louise was a pain in the ass when it came to the house. It was a nice house, but a house was a house, and living was always more important than possessing things and keeping those possessions tidy. There seemed no pleasing Louise when it came to the house. Louise thought Fiona was a complete slob, which seemed frightening considering her friends thought she was a neat freak. She didn't compare to Louise. But we all have our things, Fiona thought, and she took her reprimands with humor. If Louise thought she was a slob, she was a slob.

When all were clean and straightened, they sat at the elegant, marble-topped dining table with the candelabra and Waterford crystal. Jane was neatly attired in her dinner shirt. Thankfully, Claudette had warned Adrienne to bring a nice shirt. Claudette told her that they loved Louise dearly but she was extremely anal. In fact, she took anal to new heights.

"So we're watching our p's and q's" Adrienne asked.

"To keep strife to the minimum, yes," Claudette responded.

Adrienne did notice that Fiona got away with khaki shorts, but her white silk blouse was impeccably pressed. The shorts were nice because with legs like that it would be a shame to lose them in fabric, which was probably why Louise allowed them at the dinner table. Claudette was right. Louise was anal.

During most of dinner Adrienne found herself lost in admiration of someone else's wife. She tried hard not to stare, but she had license when Fiona engaged Jane in some political discussion. Motives are a scary thing, Adrienne thought, watching the two sisters battling opposite positions and contemplating her own sudden lust for married woman.

The sisters definitely both had the same fiery temperament and strong beliefs. It was a pity their focus veered off to such different paths. They would have been a formidable force together. But opposition was nothing new. They'd all crossed party lines before. Fiona had chosen scholastic theory, while Jane moved with force and an in-your-face aplomb that was difficult to get around. Fiona thought it detrimental to shove political action down people's throats. Jane retorted that books and theory only matter to people who read them and are already won over.

"Convincing the already convinced is redundant, Fiona. You like it because it's neat and clean and no one gets hurt. Life's not like that. Get slapped enough times, and you'll fight back," Jane said.

"Well, let's give it a rest and have brandy on the deck. It's a beautiful night. Shall we, ladies?" Louise said, wetting her fingers in her water glass and snuffing out the candles.

Adrienne eased into a chair with her brandy and thought about what Jane had said. Her motives for joining Defenders had not been so noble. She wanted to get out of the house and away from her girlfriend. She was suffering the lesbian if-I-go-you-go syndrome of codependence. She'd reached her breaking point.

She had stood in the cold, fighting against the wind, staring at the kiosk outside the student center. She wasn't looking for anything in particular. She was trying to numb herself, wondering if a bout of pneumonia would take her mind off her girlfriend troubles.

The weather mimicked her mood, making her

think of those awful James Fenimore Cooper novels filled with the exploits of Natty Bumppo. What sort of a fucking name was that? Under most circumstances she loved lit class, but this semester she felt academia had stretched the limits of good taste and the professor was a perfectly horrid man. His infatuation with Cooper skirted homoerotic, necrophilic behavior. Cooper was god — no argument.

Adrienne felt nauseated every time she walked through the classroom door. But the weather thing stuck with her. It was trite and mundane, yet she found herself painting moods with swirls of clouds, feeling bright on sunny days and chaotic or blue when the blustery weather of fall took hold. The insidious bastard had won. There was no cure.

The light that afternoon reminded her of those daytime dramas with their eerie sets, a world perpetually half in and half out of twilight. An indecisive light, one of promise or defeat, but never stepping enough in one direction or the other.

Adrienne knew the subtleness of the soap operas because Jane made her watch them for hours. Jane was studying how they affected the subconscious of the women who were hooked on them. She was convinced the government was behind them, using them as a form of mind control. She got off on some weird tangent of LSD-induced mind waves or some such nonsense. Luckily, her advisor got her back on track and she ended up with a brilliant master's thesis.

Studying the poster advertising the meeting for dyke rights, Adrienne had had no idea that she would meet someone like Jane, that she would watch soap operas for days and have the most incredible conversations about everything under the sun with this woman who seemed like a crazy genius. She was the woman who gave her the courage to walk out on lesbian longevity, learning she could still be a good lesbian and not feel the need to cohabit.

It would take quite the woman to get her to do that again. Of course she still heard Bel telling her, "Yeah, all the newly divorced say that, give it some time and you'll be ready to hook up the U-Haul and move wife number three right in." "I won't, Bel, I swear," Adrienne told her. "Twenty bucks" Adrienne bet her, knowing somehow she'd lose.

The only reason she had gone to the meeting was to piss Julia off because Adrienne was sick of having such a short leash. She knew Julia wouldn't go. She could have time alone, and she needed it desperately. Adrienne was to the point of gasping for air. Imminent suffocation was looming around the corner. She had to do something and she had to do it quick. She went, met Jane, and then the trouble started. Adrienne didn't regret the trouble Jane created. It cured her of the inertia threatening to swallow her.

It was good not having to think about going home, because she no longer had one. Jane said she could stay with them as long as she liked. And right now she was listening to this incredible woman speak beautifully on a half dozen topics. Adrienne was mesmerized.

Louise inevitably stopped anything that got ugly by briskly changing the subject. She should have married a politician. She maneuvered a dinner party with incredible finesse. A truly skilled hostess, Adrienne thought.

The stars were out, and Claudette gave her

rendition of the constellations. Fiona quizzed them on their summer plans for Defenders.

"The baby dykes are coming, and the introvert here is going to do a talk on direct action," Jane said, sticking an intrusive finger in Adrienne's ribs.

"Baby dykes? What's that about?" Louise asked. Sometimes Jane's dialect of intellectual slang drove her mad. It was crime against a school like Denton to crucify language in such a manner. But there was no changing Jane. Lord knows she'd tried.

Fiona smiled and translated. "Junior members of the select team of Dyke Defenders."

"Exactly," Jane said. "We are planning an incredible summer of blowing the conservative, motherfucking, bourgeois bastards right the fuck out of the water."

Adrienne watched Louise blanch.

"Quite the invective. Is that how you begin your seminars?" Louise inquired, alarmed at Jane's use of the English language. Louise suspected that Jane considered her part of the perverted, bourgeois power structure she so adamantly despised. Louise had visions of Jane's storm troopers armed with torches coming to burn down her beautiful house because it was beautiful and thus a thing to be destroyed. Louise never did understand the premise of Jane's politics, but they seemed fraught with danger and a certain animosity toward money, power, and beauty. How else could you explain cutting your hair in such a perverse manner and living in hovels in the city? It made no sense. Jane's father had left her a healthy trust fund that she refused to touch.

But Fiona swore there was absolutely nothing she could do to change Jane's mind. Louise suspected that

Fiona didn't want to try. It was a family conspiracy. Jane needed to grow up, and it had become a mission in Louise's life to change Jane's mind. And this sleeping-around business would have to stop. Either you were with a person, body and soul, or you weren't. You couldn't be half in the bag, half out. It was offensive to the order of the universe. We must have order, Louise thought, or life will crumble into anarchy. And anarchy was beastly. Order, we must have order. Sometimes she felt like a judge in a courtroom full of jesters.

Louise put her thoughts neatly to rest with a small sigh and a swish of her shoulders. Fiona was well acquainted with Louise's gestures, and she knew her wife had had enough of their company. Louise relinquished her role of hostess and went to bed. Fiona would join her shortly. They, too, had some things to sort out. Everything was not as it appeared. Fiona told her the planets were in retrograde, which caused unrest in the universe.

"Where did you pick up that hogwash?"

"Margo told me."

"Your crazy friend would be into astrology. Next she'll be doing your chart."

"She already has."

"What does the illustrious future hold?" Louise asked snidely.

"Don't ask."

"I won't."

"Coming up soon?" Louise asked.

"Yes, I'll get the girls settled and be up shortly."

"All right. There are extra blankets in the linen closet. I hadn't counted on a third houseguest."

"You know how spontaneous Jane is."

"All too aware," Louise said, over her shoulder.

"Good night, dear."

"Soon?"

"Very."

Fiona had spent the last week at her mother's, which gave them both much-needed space. They hadn't fought, necessarily. Rather, a few sharp words had passed between them. A couple of days of silence, then the well-thought-out discussion ensued. Politesse and decorum through and through. Sometimes Fiona wanted to scream and shake Louise into some action, tears, true words; to tumble the facade of good behavior; to initiate something rough, coming to some conclusion; to scream I love you, I hate you, anything real, hard, and true. As Louise climbed the stairs, Fiona thought, I love you but I can't keep living in this vacuum of love and commitment. I want to fight, talk, cry, make up, and make love. Start over. Anything but this stasis of good behavior.

Fiona got the guests settled and went upstairs to find Louise sitting on the bed drying her hair, her white robe opened loosely at the throat. Fiona smiled and felt color rising in her face. She wanted to nestle her face in those lovely breasts and suckle their warmth, but she knew better. Louise couldn't be ravished into making love. She had to be coaxed, gently. Sex was something a little too raw for Louise's refined nature. This didn't help Fiona's attitude of wanting to thump her bones, of wanting to take her roughly, ardently, to take her places she'd never let herself go, to take her over the edge to total abandon, to make her want and want so bad she'd let go and let Fiona break through, to feel her, know her, touch her.

Louise smiled back. Fiona felt herself grow warm, wondering if once again she would be disappointed, the endless teenage-boy syndrome, always hoping this time she'd get laid. Would tonight be the night she'd get lucky? She hated herself for feeling this way. She hated Louise for being stingy, for controlling the storehouse of love. She hated herself for always wanting and seldom getting.

Fiona crawled in bed behind her.

"Dinner was wonderful."

"Thank you, darling."

Fiona gently combed the tangles from Louise's hair.

"I remember when you used to get so nervous, the kitchen was a disaster, and yet somehow you'd pull it off. Make it look so easy. And now you're so smooth, comfortable with it. You're a stunning hostess."

"Do you miss those times?" Louise asked, thinking back to their college days.

"Sometimes," Fiona said, nestling her face in Louise's neck. She was thinking of those sultry spring days lying naked together in the living room making love in the afternoon after class. Days when they couldn't get enough of each other.

"What do you miss most?" Louise asked, turning to stroke Fiona's face.

"You," Fiona said, knowing she wasn't able to mask the desire shining in her eyes.

Louise kissed her softly, then ardently. Fiona reached gently inside Louise's robe and slowly kissed her breasts. Louise unbuttoned Fiona's blouse and removed it, letting the silk slide down her shoulders. She kissed Fiona's long, delicate neck. Fiona melted.

* * * * *

Adrienne couldn't get settled enough to sleep. She crept out into the living room. She sat in the quiet moonlight that flooded the wood floor from the bay windows. It was a lovely house. She tried imagining what Fiona looked like in the throes of passion. She hadn't meant to listen, but sliding past their bedroom door she heard the soft cries and low moans of women making love.

It was difficult fitting Louise into the scene. No amount of conjuring made it right. Louise seemed too prim and proper to engage in something so carnal, so primal. Sex was primal, base, in touch with something deep within yourself. Making love branded you with your lover, even if it was only a liaison for an evening. The marks of your lover's hands on your body stayed with you for years afterward, the thoughts of her eyes, the twisting of her body in passionate embrace, of holding you tight while she came. There was nothing like it. Love was greater than anything in the universe. The power of love . . . or was it sex? Adrienne wondered.

And those images seemed completely beyond Louise's ken. Now, Fiona was a different story. She looked like she would enjoy love, that she would relish and savor the feelings. Her long runner's legs wrapped around your body, reaching for you, needing you, wanting you.

Thinking of those two making love made Adrienne think of Julia. How those lover's hands had become the brand of a dictator. Claudette was right. She had settled for comfort when she craved passion. Passion with someone like Jane. But Jane was hard to live with. Claudette was a saint for even attempting it. Wasn't there a woman who could be both a soul mate and a lover? Was it asking too much? Was it even obtainable? Adrienne sensed she was seeking an answer she was afraid to find.

Adrienne knew for the time being she would steer clear of women. Easy enough since she was rebounding. Lesbians were leery of rebounders. Adrienne wondered how couples like Fiona and Louise did it. Louise didn't look easy to live with. But somehow they managed. Fiona must be the saint. Maybe she was one of those nearly perfect women.

Of course, those kind of women always had lovers. The older she got, the less perfect her choices became. Less amiable women with a lot of baggage, like Julia. A slew of crates filled with dusty bric-a-brac come to life, popping up their ugly little heads full of justification, needing things and understanding nothing.

Adrienne wanted a partner to love, but she did not want the run-of-the-mill-lesbian-mothering-turned-smothering routine. She always felt squeezed so tight she couldn't breathe, making her want to run and keep running, fearful to look back.

Fiona lay quivering in Louise's arms, her skin still glistening, her breathing rapid.

"The things you do to me," Fiona murmured.

"Hmm," Louise responded, pulling her close.

"I missed you, darling," Fiona said, feeling tears build up.

"Don't, please," Louise said, kissing the tears from her eyes.

"I can't help it."

"We just need some time to work out the rough spots. It'll be all right. I promise."

Louise kissed Fiona's breasts and worked her way down. Fiona felt Louise's tongue inside her. She closed her eyes. They would talk later.

Adrienne sat on the couch, her knees pulled in tight. She was meditating, taking her mind deep inside until she could almost feel herself being pulled inside out. It was a feeling that she was getting closer and closer to perfecting. She had learned it as a child when her parents were fighting. She would plug her ears and think about going inside herself to a place where she was safe and no one could hurt her, a place where her father's rage and her mother's tears did not exist, a place where things didn't get broken or bruised.

She heard a soft noise behind her. Fiona was pouring herself a glass of bottled water. Adrienne pulled out slowly. Coming out too quickly would leave her feeling discombobulated for hours afterward. She had learned this from experience, from the times when Julia would scream at her and shake her. She turned to see Fiona in a T-shirt. Adrienne should have been polite and averted her eyes, but she didn't. Instead, her eyes caressed the loveliest rear end she had ever seen. A runner's butt. She was going to have to take up jogging so she could worship with Amazons.

* * * * *

Louise had fallen asleep in Fiona's arms, and
Fiona had listened to Louise's even breathing, studied
her face, stroked it with a lover's touch, enjoyed the
sense of peace sleep brings. But she couldn't sleep.
She was still anxious from a week spent worrying
about the state of a relationship that had once seemed
so strong, so unbreakable.

She felt fragile. Fiona couldn't imagine life without
Louise in it. She kept wondering if she was going to
have to, and then there was the Internet screen name
written on the cover of a magazine, a woman from
one of the lesbian chat rooms. She couldn't imagine
Louise approaching one of those tainted places.

But there was the screen name, and Fiona checked
her profile. It wasn't a business acquaintance. She
hadn't meant to be the peering wife, but she was
curious and now nervous. She kept thinking about
how loving someone, even for a long time, didn't
necessarily guarantee that you knew her, that she
didn't have a secret life. Fiona had never had the
desire to have a secret life, but plenty of her friends
did. Anything was possible.

And then this strange need for space, how quite
suddenly Fiona's schedule had become a source of
irritation for Louise. She didn't like her running or
working late hours at the office when a deadline was
due. Sacred things. Never mess with a runner's
passion. Lovers come and go, but not running.
Running was an addiction no twelve-step program
could cure. Running kept her sane. Asking her to quit
was like asking for her very soul. No one had the
right to ask that or to think she could.

* * * * *

Fiona saw Adrienne curled up into a ball on the couch.

"Can't sleep?"

"No, and I hate to toss and turn. I'd rather get up and try again later," Adrienne said.

"Me too. Is it because you're in a strange house?"

"No. I've never been in one place long enough to develop that particular phobia."

"Do you want to try my late-night tonic that is specially designed to induce sleep?" Fiona asked.

"Does it really work?"

"That depends on your level of belief," Fiona said, smiling.

"Do you want to go to all that trouble?" Adrienne said.

"What else do we have to do at this time of night?"

"True."

Fiona set to work. Adrienne came to help. They got to giggling as they tried to be quiet.

"Shh, Louise will come down, and there'll be hell to pay," Fiona warned as a cascade of clattering pans came down on Adrienne. "Your kitchen privileges have been revoked. Take a seat."

Fiona maneuvered her to a stool. Adrienne felt her touch acutely. Her hands were smooth and cool. Their eyes met briefly and Adrienne looked away quickly.

"So you do talk," Fiona chided, as they sat sipping the mysterious sleeping concoction.

"Sometimes," Adrienne replied shyly.

"It's okay being quiet. We can't all be talkers,

think how noisy the world would be. All that noise and no one quiet long enough to hear it."

"You talk beautifully. I get nervous and forget what I wanted to say, or I get it all muddled. I don't know how I'm going to do those Zap sessions. I know I'll freeze up," Adrienne said.

"I'm not the extrovert I appear. I know my audience. I feel a lot more vulnerable elsewhere. Maybe that's what is keeping you up."

"Could be. Stage fright. Brings back college days. I think I suffered sleep deprivation the whole time. My mother would be so disappointed with me during break because I slept the whole time."

"And she wanted to go out shopping and have lunch."

"Yes. Why do mothers always want to do that kind of stuff?"

"It must be their idea of female bonding," Fiona said.

"Ugh!"

"My sentiments exactly."

"Mine thinks if she takes me into enough women's departments I'll start liking men. You know, buy a dress and all that," Adrienne said, feeling her shoulders tense up with the thought of a weekend spent at home. She tried to crack her neck. If only she could learn to relax. She swore to herself that when she graduated from college she'd take up yoga or something. Treat her body right.

Fiona poured them both another dose.

"You're not relaxing."

"I know."

"Here," Fiona said, coming up behind her. She gently kneaded Adrienne's neck and shoulders.

Adrienne closed her eyes, liking the contact, the closeness, Fiona's strong hands kneading her body, sensing what her body wanted.

"So why can't you sleep? Big race coming up?"

"I don't run competitively. I run to keep my head clear," Fiona said, knowing she had answered only half the question. How could she tell this stranger that she was falling out of love with her wife, that she felt sad and lonely, and that she ran to get away from those feelings? When she ran she felt whole again, felt her soul trying to catch the wind and travel with it to a faraway place where she would no longer hurt. A place where pain didn't live. A place where she could be free.

"Feel better?" Fiona asked.

"Yes, much. Thank you."

"Can you sleep?"

"I think so," Adrienne said.

"Let's try then. Now that I know you can talk, perhaps we should have coffee someday and you can tell me stories."

"What kind of stories?"

"The kind with happy endings," Fiona teased.

"What if I don't know any?" Adrienne asked seriously.

"Then you'll have to make them up."

Adrienne watched Fiona climb the stairs, knowing she had quite suddenly fallen in love with those beautiful legs.

Two

Adrienne sat having coffee at the neighborhood café waiting for Jane, who was notorious for being tardy. Punctuality was another form of control, and Jane saw it as her civil duty to buck its reign. Watches were tedious. Jane adhered solely to her natural rhythms. When she needed a café au lait she'd show. Adrienne didn't mind the wait. It gave her time to daydream of Fiona. Her new pastime.

Every moment of the weekend lingered in the corners of her mind and she replayed the moments often. She memorized the details so she wouldn't forget a single nuance — every look, smile, move of the hand, her touch, her legs, the flush of her face after a run. Adrienne knew it was an absurd waste of time, but she couldn't help it.

She was dreaming of another woman's wife, her best friend's sister, a woman so far beyond her reach it was ludicrous to think Fiona would give her a second thought. But the daydreams persisted and the vision intensified. Adrienne found herself unable to stop either. In the back of her mind she knew she'd lasted about four hours without becoming infatuated. So much for leaving love alone for a while. Her heart had the attention span of a two-year-old in a roomful of toys.

Jane flounced in, flirted briefly with the waitress, got her coffee, and sat down, smiling devilishly at Adrienne.

"You look absolutely stunning."

"Why, thank you," Adrienne said, affecting a Southern accent.

You know what I'd really like to do?" Jane said, leaning in closer.

"No, what?"

"Spend the afternoon fucking your brains out."

Adrienne blushed. "I don't think that's such a good idea with Benton Peugh's arrival looming on the horizon and no plan in sight. Do you?"

"Raincheck?"

"Perhaps."

"Are you done with me?" Jane said, pouting.

"I highly doubt I'll ever be done with you."

"Good," Jane said, a smile creeping across her face. She squeezed Adrienne's thigh, closed her eyes, and sighed.

"What are you thinking?"

"How you feel when I'm inside you."

"Jane!"

"You know I'm a hedonist first, political activist second."

"And you're dangerous on both counts," Adrienne said.

"Thank you, darling. You always say just the right thing. How can I resist you? But you're right. We must come up with a plan or our nemesis will surely steal the show. We need something big, really big."

"Have you seen those little green cards the opposition have been sending out?"

"What cards?"

"Hasn't Mary the news junkie filled you in on that yet?"

"You know why her eyesight is so bad. It's all the television, sitting in front of the blinking box, taking in those vibes, letting them permeate her soul. To the point of addiction. She'll probably have a child one day and park it for hours at a time before the almighty telly god and have it educated, feeding it McDonald's hamburgers and french fries until it grows up to be another massive consumer of heinous goods and services. It's sick, Adrienne. Absolutely sick."

"I remember when you parked me there for days watching those daytime soaps."

"That was research," Jane said.

"Mary is doing research."

"It's different. She worships CNN. Takes it for gospel."

"Anyway, what are we going to do?" Adrienne asked, trying to steer Jane clear of another of her favorite yet hated tangents.

"I don't know. Tell me about the green cards."

"The right-to-lifers want people to send them to their local congressperson to stop late-term abortion. They make it sound like doctors are yanking nearly grown babies from the snatches of irresponsible women who are using abortion as a form of birth control."

"Are they?"

"The fetuses are late term."

"Is there a color brochure to accompany the card?"

"No."

"Good. We'll have Mary do some more research."

"And in the meantime?" Adrienne asked.

"We'll think. Do we have the agenda for Peugh's visit yet? We definitely need a high-pressure Zap with full media coverage."

"It's being faxed from headquarters compliments of our latest spy," Adrienne said.

"Wouldn't Peugh just shit if he knew that a lesbian in a pink gingham dress is really a Dyke Defender in disguise keeping us up-to-date on all his moves. You'd think for such an intelligent man he'd wonder how it is that we show up at every single one of his freak shows."

"It's a testimony to the extent of his focus. He thinks of nothing else," Adrienne replied.

"I'm meeting Fiona later to discuss some hideous financial venture. My trust fund, you know. You want to come? Maybe we can pick her brains."

"I wish. Tonight is my night with the baby dykes. Direct action moves," Adrienne said. "How is she?" she continued, trying to conceal the blush she felt rising by hiding behind her menu.

"I don't know. I think something's up. She hasn't said anything, but she spent last week at Mother's. No one spends time at the homestead unless they've been thrown out."

"But Louise behaves like the perfect partner."

"Precisely. How would you like to live with a Martha Stewart clone? It's got to be tedious sometimes. All those perfect dinners. I mean, come on. What's wrong with the occasional salad bar — guzzle a little beer, smoke a cig, let it all get loose. Fiona never gets to do that, and I think secretly she craves it. We'll have to drag her out one night. Teach her to party with the gals. Okay, I better get going while my caffeine buzz is still peaking," Jane said, slapping her Rollerblades on, sailing past the waitress and plucking an olive from the top of a Greek salad.

The waitress smiled. A new conquest perhaps? Adrienne wondered. Jane waved as she rolled past the window, flashing Adrienne a tit and a smile. One day she was going to get arrested for indecent exposure. Nothing new.

Fiona sat having lunch with her mother.

"How are things going?" Hazel asked, dipping her fork gingerly into the antipasto.

"Tentative at best."

"Meaning?" Hazel inquired further.

"Meaning, I feel unresolved, lost, slightly negligent without knowing why. Nervous and pressured to do something, only I don't know what it would be," Fiona said, picking at her salad.

"Do you have any idea what brought this on?"

"You mean why Louise is suddenly unhappy with my personal habits?"

"Yes," Hazel said, taking a sip of wine.

"I don't know," Fiona answered, wondering if the cause of Louise's unrest had something to do with the woman on the Internet.

"Are either one of you straying?"

"Straying?"

"Having an affair," Hazel said, looking intently at Fiona with a matching pair of topaz eyes.

"I'm not. I wouldn't know what to do."

"There's not much to do. It usually just happens and then you sort out how you feel after you've committed the error."

"Is it always an error?" Fiona asked.

"Not necessarily, but in most cases it is."

"Did you ever cheat on Dad?"

Hazel refilled both their glasses with a dark burgundy. She had never told anyone about that strange semester with the visiting Italian professor.

She could still feel the strong muscles of his back as he moved his body against hers. Those hot afternoons they'd spent fucking and how she would go home, shower off her lover's caresses and smells, and once again become the dutiful wife to a man who never suspected her of such an indiscretion.

No one ever would, and she supposed that was what made it so easy. Too easy until she thought she would burst from the grand size of the secret like a communion wafer soaked in wine expanding in her throat. And the day her lover left, begging her to come with him, and how they both knew she couldn't. The tears she cried in the bath as she washed the last vestiges of his caresses from her body, knowing she would never again feel his touch, smell his breath, taste his flesh.

And then they wrote letters, though they swore they wouldn't. One afternoon going through her mail she saw his familiar scrawl blazing like his smile across the front of an envelope. There followed months of writing letters until she had stacks of them. It was their secret life, until one day when something changed. Changed in her.

She remembered Charles coming to pick her up at the office. They were going out to dinner. She knew he was coming before he knocked on her door. She heard his firm footsteps climbing the stairs to her turret office, the best office on campus: she had rescued it from becoming a janitorial storage space, and it became her refuge.

She knew students came to see her sometimes just to look out the little windows across the tree-strewn campus and breathe fresh air fluttering through the curtains. Her office was the only place on campus that didn't smell dank, and she always had fresh-cut flowers, classical music, baked goods, and espresso. It was a civilized place, and her students respected it as such. No ill manners were tolerated, and for a few moments they would sit and feel human.

Charles had brought her flowers, and she slipped the last letter from Italy in her drawer before she looked up and smiled at her husband. He looked handsome in his suit, his face tanned from afternoons spent gardening. He leaned down and kissed her on the cheek and quite suddenly she fell back in love with him. That night they went home and made love, and it felt good to be in his familiar, secure arms. He knew just how to please her, and he was gently concerned for her passion. And she knew then she would give up her Italian lover.

The next day she wrote her lover one last letter, with only the word *good-bye*. She never had another lover, and she was glad. It made him special, and in a strange way he taught her how to fall in love again with her husband. She couldn't tell him that, but she hoped he knew.

Thinking back to the last days of the affair, she remembered beginning to crave the normalcy of her life before the affair. She had always wondered about being a wife and mother and having a lover to stave off the boredom of married life as it began to creep up on her.

She remembered oscillating between the two men, feeling strange for experiencing neither guilt nor remorse but only a kind of fulfillment at having both of them. Days when life seemed full and she felt happy, felt glowing with a sensuality she felt she'd lost, a passion her life suddenly regained. And people noticed. She would smile.

Were these the things she should tell Fiona? How could she explain to Fiona that having a lover made her love Charles more, that she could once again see his good traits, the things he possessed that made her love him in the first place when those traits were laid next to her lover's?

Tell her to get herself a lover and she'll find she likes Louise better, or maybe she won't. Maybe the lover will take her away, give her back her passion and she'll live quite happily with someone new. Maybe for her the craving won't stop, maybe it will consume her and she'll be forced to choose, or Louise might discover her indiscretion. Hazel wondered what Charles would have done had he found out. Would she have begged his forgiveness or would she have packed, leaving him with the babies, and gone off to Italy?

"I think sometimes people need a vacation from each other, a breather if you will, time to find themselves again. Taking some space for yourself doesn't mean you want out, necessarily. It could be a new beginning," Hazel said, taking a piece of bread from the basket.

"Louise won't see it that way. She'll see it as betrayal."

"Teach her to see it that way. Do it gradually. A night out with the girls. It would do you both good," Hazel replied.

"I thought we were so strong nothing like this could happen to us. I can't believe we're having trouble."

"Why? Because only other people have trouble? Don't be vain, Fiona. Relationships are always in a state of flux. Nothing is guaranteed."

"I suppose you're right."

"Of course I'm right, darling. I'm your mother. Mothers are supposed to be right. Now tell me about this midnight chat you had with Jane's new friend, Adrienne."

"How did you know?"

"Jane told me. Baby sisters make the best spies."

"There's not much to tell."

"Tell me anyway."

* * * * *

"Yeah, well, who the fuck do you think you are? Landlords are not synonymous with God. Take a hike, you miserable little fuck," Jane screamed as she slammed the door. The baby dykes looked at her with eyes big as saucers.

Adrienne glanced up from the sign she was painting.

"We'd better get packing. Twenty bucks says there will be an eviction notice taped to the door tomorrow. You know, Jane, with your temper office space is getting more and more difficult to find," Claudette said, standing up and stretching.

"I can't fucking believe it. Total bullshit, utter and complete bullshit," Jane said, slamming the door again for emphasis.

"What did you do this time?" Claudette asked.

"It's the fucking tits again, and he doesn't like the mannequin parts sticking out of the Dumpsters. He says we're making it uncomfortable for the other clientele. Other clientele. What fucking clientele? A bunch of lowlife wanna-be artists who do nothing but smoke cigarettes all day and talk about how mistreated they are. They don't do anything about it. They just sit and bitch," Jane said.

"Tits?" Sarah inquired.

"Haven't you seen the women's rest room lately? It's incredible, simply incredible," Mary said.

"Go look," Jane said.

"Jane's ongoing sculpture in worship of breasts," Adrienne said.

"Does the fucking landlord know how many

Dumpsters I had to dive into to get that many breasts? It's hard work," Jane said.

"Yes, it is hard work, and we're awfully proud of you," Claudette said.

Sarah came back truly awed by the experience.

"It's beautiful, all those breasts hanging from the ceiling."

Jane smiled at her. Up to this point she'd dubbed Sarah "Stupid Girl." Of course, the last time they'd met Jane had to be physically restrained from throttling her when she told them that hate was such a negative concept. Jane shuddered, thinking the New Agers would have to go, the bunch of naive herbivores with their stupid crystals and Goddess nonsense. She needed focused people in the movement, not vortex-worshiping idiots.

"That does it. I'm buying the fucking building. Joining the bourgeois. Next I'll be driving a Beemer and shopping at Saks," Jane said.

"What building?" Adrienne asked.

"The one Fiona wants me to buy. She says we can use it for office space as well as living quarters — with the right permits, of course. But she said she'd take care of that nonsense. I don't think she trusts me when it comes to dealing with the political machine."

"I can't imagine why. Take a look at your police record," Adrienne said.

"You have a police record?" Sarah said, obviously astonished.

"Yes, I murdered one or two already-brain-dead people out of sheer frustration with the fact that they were using aerosol deodorants despite the widening gap in the ozone," Jane said.

"You mean like Dr. Kevorkian?" Sarah asked,

trying to create a picture in her head of Jane with a white gown and an angelic expression on her face.

"I'm gonna fucking kill her," Jane said, moving in Sarah's direction.

"Jane, stop it!" Claudette commanded. Jane stood still.

"About the building . . ." Adrienne prodded.

"Yeah, well I got to do something with Dad's money or the IRS is going to suck it up. So I buy this dilapidated building and we fix things. My friends have a safe, better place to live; we have office space that no one can evict us from; and in exchange for organizing it all Fiona gets the top floor for her office space as soon as her lease is up. I can use the rent profits to supplement my income so that I can fully devote myself to the movement and quit my lowlife jobs, although I am rather attached to some of them, and everything turns out peachy-keen," Jane said, mimicking Fiona's words practically verbatim.

"And just how much does a building cost?" Adrienne asked, unable to comprehend how one would even entertain the idea of doing such a thing.

"Not as much as you would think. It was an old warehouse, then studios, then nothing, I guess. Anyway, no one appears to want the thing, which means the bastard who owns it will take anything. Fiona, the financial genius, will probably get it for a song and make me a land baron in the process," Jane said.

"Just don't become a slumlord," Adrienne said.

"Yeah, smoking fat cigars and ripping off poor people from the back of my white limo on the way to lunch with a city official," Jane said, wrapping her arms around Adrienne.

47

Adrienne looked at Jane quizzically.

"I would never," Jane swore.

"Okay, then buy the thing," Adrienne said, looking back over her shoulder at Jane and then past her to Sarah, who stood puzzled by Jane's apparent intimacy with Adrienne in front of Claudette. The Dyke Defenders were definitely going to broaden this suburban girl's horizons, Adrienne thought.

"It's all so tedious," Jane said.

There was a pounding on the door, and when Jane opened it she found the eviction notice nailed to the door.

"Have you ever noticed how the universe takes one thing away and then gives you something else in exchange? Like maybe things are planned and what you got you needed more than what you lost," Jane said, wadding the eviction notice into a ball, scoring two points with the waste can, and walking out of the room, feeling suddenly philosophical and needing to go on one of her Walt Whitman walks about the city.

They stood silent for a moment.

"She's a genius," Sarah said.

Adrienne shook her head and went back to painting her protest sign.

"Does she tire you out sometimes?" Adrienne asked Claudette after they'd both had time to think.

"Often, but she also excites me with her joie d'esprit. She thinks a lot and I like that, because she makes me think in return," Claudette replied. "Maybe not a genius, but definitely bright."

Mary smiled, looking up from her clippings. Sarah was too engrossed in her sign to hear the discussion.

* * * * *

Claudette and Adrienne decided to go for Chinese food and then go see the latest romantic lesbian flick, the kind of movie Jane wouldn't be caught dead at.

"Even dedicated direct activists need some diversion once in a while," Adrienne said, feeling guilty.

"Don't justify pleasure. When we do that it allows the Puritanical forefathers a foothold in our psychological makeup."

"A Jane-made syllogism?" Adrienne asked.

"But of course."

"Do we get a big bag of popcorn?" Adrienne asked.

"Only if you'll hold hands in the bad parts," Claudette said, smiling.

"I'll hold your hand in good parts, too, if you'd like," Adrienne said. "You know, I find you extremely restful."

"In stark contrast to Jane?" Claudette asked.

"Yes."

"I'm glad."

Sarah watched this whole display with a peculiar look on her face.

"Mary?" Sabina asked when they were alone.

"Yes," Mary said, removing her thick glasses and rubbing her eyes.

"Is Adrienne sleeping with both Claudette and Jane?"

"I don't think she's sleeping with either one of them at the moment."

"Well, don't you think they're awfully touchy-feely with one another?"

"I think it's more like sisterly affection, and even if it is more it's really none of our business," Mary replied.

"But haven't Jane and Claudette been together for a long time?"

"Yes," Mary answered tentatively, knowing full well where this was leading.

"Kind of like married, right?"

"Yes."

"So why are they fooling around with other people?" Sarah asked.

"They have a slightly different view on monogamy."

"Like what?" Sarah asked.

"More open, I guess. They're happy. That's all that counts, right?"

"I'm not so sure. Mary, why doesn't Jane like me?"

Mary put her glasses back on. Sarah stopped being a blur and came into focus. She thought for a moment. She couldn't say, "Because you're stupid. Maybe not stupid, but you just don't think before you open your mouth. Or maybe it's that you're a little slow to grasp things." It was just as hard to be smart as it was to be stupid. People had trouble dealing with you either way. She looked at Sarah's large green eyes and dark wispy hair and thought, At least you have looks on your side. All I have is smarts, but that doesn't get me laid, and I bet you get laid a lot.

"Jane is very intense. She doesn't mean to be harsh; it just comes out that way. She'll warm up to you soon. Don't worry about it," Mary said, thinking, If she doesn't kill you first. It would be a mercy killing, one less person taking up precious space. There really are too many people, Mary thought. Perhaps we should borrow all the children being warehoused in day care, state care, and foster care and take them to the capital so that the legislature could see what their handiwork was accomplishing — more unwanted children growing up to be unfulfilled, fucked-up adults creating more unwanted children.

"I wish I was smart like you," Sarah said.

Mary blushed. "But you'd probably be homely too. Can't have everything."

"I don't think you're homely. I think you're cute."

"In an academic way," Mary said, turning back to her computer.

"No, just cute in your own way. You want to go grab a pizza?"

"I don't know. I've got lots to do," Mary said.

"We could get pizza and I could come back and help you."

Mary was quiet, trying to figure out how to get out of this one.

"Come on," Sarah said, putting on her best pleading look.

"All right. But then I really must come back and get some work done."

"I'll help if you let me," Sarah said, looking like a puppy dog that got its way.

Three

"You talked her into doing what?" Louise asked, removing the croissants from the oven. Her apron was lightly dusted with flour and, unbeknownst to her, she had a smudge of flour across her cheek.

Fiona would have liked to kiss her, but she was in trouble. There would be no kissing. At the rate things were going, she'd be sleeping in the guest room.

"Maybe I'll go for my run and fill you in on the details during dinner," Fiona suggested.

"You and that running," Louise mumbled.

"Don't," Fiona said, feeling color rising in her face.

"I'm sorry. Go running. We'll talk later."

"What's happening to us?" Fiona asked.

"Nothing, darling. Go. We'll talk after dinner, civilly."

"Okay."

Fiona did her stretches and took off, knowing already her pace was too fast and she would pay later. Right now she didn't care. She wanted to get away from Louise, the house, her life. I am thirty-eight years old and I hate my life, she thought. I sound like some barbaric teenager on a rampage through the mall, angry at everything and everyone. Just breathe, concentrate on your breathing, she told herself.

She listened to the even thud of her shoes on the pavement and the grass as she cut across Loring Park and headed toward the university. She tried to envision shedding her bad feelings like a cape behind her, leaving them scattered for the wind to pick and take to new places. She often wondered where all the bad thoughts went on the stream of wind.

Was there some place, some forlorn corner of the universe where bad things resided? What sort of a place would it be that housed all that was let go, all the malicious, ugly things people like herself sloughed off to keep their sanity. When we let go of bad things, when we finally learn to let go of them, where do they go? Is it possible they disappear without a trace, or is the negativity recirculated? Fiona shuddered at the thought. How and where did Louise put her bad things?

She stopped at the light just before the bridge, running in place to keep her heart rate up. Adrienne stood across the street, watching for the light to change. Fiona was lost in her thoughts and nearly ran past her when Adrienne recognized the woman she'd been thinking of for weeks.

"Hey," Adrienne said, touching Fiona's arm.

Fiona looked over. She stopped.

"Hello," Fiona said, smiling briefly. They stood for a moment looking at each other as the other passersby went around them.

Fiona walked with Adrienne to the other side.

"I have a story to tell you," Adrienne lied.

"You do? Does it have a happy ending?"

"Yes. Will you have coffee someday still?" Adrienne asked.

"And when would this someday be?" Fiona teased.

"Whenever you'd like."

"Tomorrow at five."

"Sure," Adrienne said, feeling herself blush.

"How about the Walker Café?" Fiona suggested.

"Perfect."

Fiona took off running leaving Adrienne standing watching her go, admiring her legs, and feeling like this was truly her lucky day.

But what sort of a story would she tell? It would have to be a good one, not boring, not funny, not trite. Something serious, something meant to impress. Adrienne had constructed and reconstructed this coffee hour in her head countless times, trying to perfect every aspect. But now that it was going to happen, all her preparations were about to scatter in complete and utter terror. She was petrified. How can I possibly expect to entertain Martha Stewart's wife? I should have just let her run past and continued to lust in secret.

The tiny voice in the back of her head said to her, You're not living if you're not taking chances. But chances are frightening, she thought. So? said the voice. So I guess I'm going for coffee. Good. Tiny voices in your head are oftentimes tedious, Adrienne thought. And cowards are boring, the voice replied. Guess you told me. I did, the voice agreed. Now get thinking of a story. Adrienne wandered off in the direction of the library.

Jane was searching the Internet for information on direct action tactics of perverse degrees. It never hurt to expand upon something that had already proved successful. Mary's computer hummed along happily, scanning the rest of the world for sites of glorious political activity. Jane waited as the computer traveled. She longed for a cigarette, but having smoked her last one over an hour ago she would have to suffer until she ran to the corner store. She was hoping someone would come by and give her one. Sandra Davis walked in with a bad hairdo. It was the first thing Jane noticed. The tip-off was the razor and cord she was dragging behind her.

"Jane, oh my god I'm so glad you're here. This is awful, perfectly awful. You've got to help me. Please."

"Sand, have you got a cig? I'm jonesing bad."

"Jane, how can you be so insensitive at a time like this?" Sandra asked, digging in her bag for the crumpled pack of Marlboros.

"Easily, I'm an addict. You know they say cigs are worse than heroin," Jane said, lighting the cigarette and taking a long drag. "Damn, that's good."

"Jane!"

"What happened to your hair?" Jane asked, suddenly making a connection between the razor and Sandra's distraught face.

"Janice started to cut it, and then things got ugly."

"What kind of things?"

"I was confessing to a few minor indiscretions."

"My god, she cut off your tail. That was years of work," Jane said, walking around Sandra and surveying the damage.

"Yeah, well, lesson learned — do not argue with your girlfriend while she's cutting your hair."

"What were you arguing about?" Jane said, mooching another cigarette and cleaning leftover hair fibers from the electric clippers.

"I told her about my little liaison with Lisa while she was away."

"How long was Janice gone?"

"Long enough," Sandra said, flouncing down on the couch.

"Why did you do it?"

"Like you should ask, the married-unmarried," Janice said.

"I like to hear other people's reasons. They're always more interesting than my own."

"God, you're a weird fuck," Sandra said, lighting her own cigarette.

"So why'd you do it?" Jane said, scooting the old coffee can they were using for an ashtray with her sneaker so it rested between the two of them.

"I guess I felt trapped, or maybe I was having a midlife crisis and needed to sow my wild oats..."

"Or maybe you were just horny and wanted something new," Jane queried, going to the fridge and raiding the last of the beer stash. She opened them both a bottle and, with a cigarette hanging from her lips, said, "I think we need one of these."

Sandra smiled. She could always count on Jane to turn a bad event into a party.

"No, I think the real reason I did it was suffocation. I felt like I was suffocating with Janice, and when she went away I felt like I could breathe again, have fun again, just fuck for the sake of fucking without all this baggage attached," Sandra replied.

"So that's all fine and dandy, but why'd you tell?"

"I don't know. I felt guilty. She came back and she'd really missed me. We had great sex and Lisa just wasn't that entertaining anymore. It was a fling for both of us, and it was over. We just kind of stopped seeing each other."

"And you wanted to absolve your sins by confessing, being the good Catholic girl you are," Jane said.

"How'd you know I was Catholic?"

"Because Catholics have the most refined, most intrusive, most highly developed sense of guilt in the entire universe. Catholics confess to having affairs. The rest of us live in fear we'll be found out, but we're never stupid enough to kiss and tell. Notice I still have hair," Jane said, pointing to her head.

"Shit, what am I going to do? It's an absolute mess," Sandra said, getting up and looking in the mirror.

"I'd say you definitely win the stupid award," Jane said.

"It just seemed like the right time. I didn't think she'd take it so hard. I didn't think it was a big deal."

"Sleeping with other women is always a big deal."

"Why is that?" Sandra said, slumping back down on the couch.

"Because we live in a fucked-up puritanical society. We can't just fuck and eat and laugh and stop all the thinking. We can't just be. There's got to be discussion and rules and definitions. Janice wanted to talk the hell out of this, didn't she? Find the ultimate reason behind it all. It couldn't just happen. There had to be a reason. You couldn't be psychotic and horny. There was some deep-seated, primordial yearning facilitating this jump in the hay," Jane said.

Sandra nodded. "I didn't know what to say to her. I just let her scream, and then she went bonkers with the clippers."

Jane sat back and surveyed the damage. "We're going to have to shave it all off. There's no way to get you even close to any anarchic sense of hair fashion. It's a botched-up mess."

"Do it then. It'll grow. Besides, I suppose I deserve it."

"Why, because you are human?" Jane said, buzzing off the remaining hair on Sandra's head.

"I guess so," Sandra said, getting nervous because Jane was dangerously close to her ear.

"Basically, you're bald," Jane said, handing Sandra the razor.

Sandra looked at her quizzically as Jane sat down. "Now shave mine."

"Why?" Sandra asked.

"Because you're my sister-in-arms, and two shaved heads are better than one."

"Jane, that's disgustingly corny."

"Why, thank you."

"You don't have to do this," Sandra said.

"No, but I want to. Look, if there're two of us, it will look like fashion. If it's only you, it will look like an accident, a bad accident, and both you and Janice will have to suffer. Get it?"

"Got it. Why do things have to be this way?" Sandra moaned, looking tentatively at Jane's head.

"For purposes of patrilineal organization."

"Patrilineal?"

"Tracing babies through their fathers. Are we going to have to start having vocabulary lessons? Wasn't it bad enough that no one knew or had heard of lesbian separatists and I had to explain it in front of a lesbian separatist, no less?"

"Who?" Sandra asked, taking a deep breath and turning the razor on.

"Griselda LeClerq, the French feminist. Weren't you at the rally?"

"I think that may have been one of those afternoons I was fucking Lisa."

"Now, extracurriculars are all right, but skipping rallies is not. Is that understood, young lady?" Jane said.

"Yes, ma'am. Actually, you don't look half bad with a shaved head. You have a very attractive skull."

"Why, thank you. So do you. Maybe this was a godsend in disguise," Jane said, rubbing her croppy stubs.

"It'll definitely cut down on bathroom time," Sandra said.

Bel Pallifa walked in and smiled at them.

"New look?"

"New look with a lot of history," Sandra replied.

"What's up?" Jane asked, surveying herself in the mirror.

"Still fighting with that prick at the bookstore," Bel responded, helping herself to a Coke and putting her boots up on the table. She was a lesbian conundrum. A young butch attired somewhere between a mechanic and a homeboy who wrote suggestive, erotic, offensive poetry that stank. Bel worked on her bad poems every day, and Jane had immense respect for her diligence. Who knew, one day bad poetry might become all the rage and Bel would be famous. Bel didn't care what people thought so long as they listened. Jane liked her shock value.

"What's his deal?" Jane asked.

"He won't let me do a reading because he says my poetry is offensive."

"What's the title of this little collection of yours?"

"It's called 'Cunts.' "

"You've got to be kidding," Sandra said, throwing Jane another cigarette and lighting herself one.

"Hum us a few bars," Jane said.

"The title piece goes like this," Bel said, standing up and filling her five-foot-eight space. She was built like a farm boy. She took a deep breath and began, "Cunts, I like cunts / like the way they smell / like the way they taste / like the way they glide beneath my touch / like them on my face / like my tongue in that space / like to be inside / like the way they ride / on my bike across town / cunts / like 'em all / big or small / cunts."

"Well, that was certainly original. But I can see how fagboy at the bookstore might find it offensive," Sandra said.

"Why there? Why not the Amazon?" Jane asked.

"I had a bit of a run-in with the owner. I've been forced to look elsewhere for my readings."

"What did you do?" Sandra asked.

"Let me guess. You took someone else's cunt for a spin around the block," Jane said.

"Just a word of advice: Never sleep with the owner's girlfriend. I've been banned from the place. Last time I went in there, Loretta threw the entire bestsellers table at me. Damn, books hurt," Bel said, rubbing her still bruised shoulder.

"Especially when they're hurled from across the room," Jane said, laughing.

"You slept with Loretta's girlfriend?" Sandy asked. "She's not even attractive."

"Cunts, I like 'em all, big or small," Bel responded.

Jane slapped her on the back. "Have I told you that you're awesome? Not like these other uptight assholes. Don't worry about the readings. Next rally, you're top billing, okay?"

"Thanks, bud."

"Hey, did I tell you I'm buying a building? You ever need a pad, a cheap one, come my way. We're going to rent out part of the space."

"Cool. Yeah, I might be looking for some new digs. The roomies are really getting hard on the drugs and drinking, and you know it's just not jiving with this clean-and-sober thing I'm doing," Bel said.

"You know, I really am proud of you. How long has it been?" Jane asked.

"Eighteen months," Bel said.

"You still go to the meetings?" Jane asked.

"Yeah, they're kind of cool. Besides, there're lots of women. Good place to meet women. And they're people trying to get their shit together, and I like that," Bel said.

"Good. Your shit's pretty much together," Jane said.

"Yeah, but I'd like to find a girl, you know, one you can go home to and have dinner with, and cuddle up to on Sunday mornings. I just haven't found the right one yet."

"Don't stop looking. She's out there," Jane said.

"Speaking of out there," Sandra said, sitting on the windowsill and blowing smoke rings out the open window.

They watched Janice come flying across the street.

"Damn!" Sandra said, sinking down onto the old couch and scrunching her eyes closed.

"There's always the fire escape," Jane suggested as they listened to the even plodding of boots on stairs.

"Perhaps we should go have a soda somewhere, Bel?" Jane queried.

"Good idea."

"Cowards," Sandra said.

"This is your pit, honey. You dug it," Jane said.

"God, I wish I was anywhere else but here," Sandra said, feeling her pulse quicken. She hated conflict. It reminded her of home, and she'd come halfway across the country to get away from a houseful of fighting family members. But the screaming and crying fits, the tired apologies, the land of kiss-and-make-up still clung like a sour odor in her car, and no amount of pine tree air fresheners could fix it. Only this time she was her father, and her girlfriends ended up being her mother, and the conflict she'd run from was now her own.

"Maybe you could click your little red shoes together and end up in Kansas," Jane chided.

"I saw the ruby slippers when I went to the Smithsonian," Bel said.

"Your knowledge base never ceases to amaze me," Jane said, opening the door for Janice, who jumped back, startled by Jane's new look until she saw Sandra. Janice burst into tears. She fell into Jane's arms as she was closest.

"It's all right, really. Time for a new hairdo anyway," Jane said, patting her gently on the back.

Janice sobbed. Jane handed her over to Sandra, who took her in her arms willingly.

"Bet they're already fucking on the couch," Jane said, slurping down the rest of her soda.

"Bet you're right. That's the only good thing about fighting. What did Sandra do, anyway?" Bel asked.

"Slept around, the usual."

"You know, that's one thing I never did. Once I'm with a gal I'm true to the end. Cause once a dog always a dog. You start that shit, and you can't stop. Some other little tasty treat comes along, and off you go. Back to lying, cheating, and stealing hearts," Bel said, nodding firmly.

"Yeah, I suppose you're right," Jane said halfheartedly.

"What about you? Seems you and Claudette got something different going on there. Never quite seen the likes of it before," Bel said.

"It's twenty-first century, basically. Sort of New Age, sort of reviving some vestiges of the sixties, the era of free love. We're together and sometimes we sleep with other people and it works."

"Cunts, gotta have 'em."

"Damn right, Bel. Read me some more stuff."

"You mean it?"

"Yeah."

Four

"Jane, you can't wear a hat at dinner. You're not supposed to wear them in the house," Louise said.

Jane rolled her eyes at Adrienne, who tried not to laugh.

"I think for everyone's benefit the hat should stay on. Come on, Louise, bend a little. I won't tell Martha," Jane said.

"Martha who?" Louise asked.

"Your goddess of husbandry, Martha Stewart."

"Oh, Martha, of course," Louise said, lightening up.

"Let her wear the hat," Fiona advised.

"Not at the dinner table. Now take it off," Louise said.

"You're not going to like it," Jane said, taking the hat off. It was a tasteful leather hat with the rainbow logo.

Louise shrieked.

Jane put the hat back on and walked out onto the patio with Adrienne gladly in tow.

"Why didn't you tell me she shaved her head?" Louise asked, slamming down a pan, sending the white, sticky roux flying.

"Because I didn't know," Fiona lied, thinking, I'm really sick of getting in trouble all the time. I am a grown woman and I shouldn't be subject to such reprimands.

"Christ, we have the most important feminist in the country coming for dinner, and we have a lobotomy patient for a dinner guest," Louise said.

Bel knocked on the back door, and Fiona let her in.

"Bel, how are you?"

"Fine, darling. Thanks for the invite. Wouldn't miss a night like tonight for anything. I brought my stuff just in case conversation moves in that direction," Bel said, tapping her leather case.

"Just not during dinner, all right?" Fiona asked.

"Sure, babe. Where are the girls?"

"Out back. Would you like a soda?" Fiona asked.

"Please."

"I'm sorry. Where are my manners?"

"Probably genetically mutated like your sister's," Louise snarled.

"Louise!"

"Now at least you know my first name. Louise Matson, nice to meet you, Bel. I hope you like chicken Kiev."

"It's my favorite," Bel lied.

Fiona led her out back.

"What's chicken Kiev?"

"Chicken with lots of goop on it," Fiona said.

"Sounds wonderful," Bel said.

"Sorry about the domestic tension," Fiona said. Bel was by far one of Fiona's favorites when it came to Jane's ragtag bunch of friends.

"Not a problem. Nice digs."

"Straight out of Martha Stewart," Fiona said.

"Bel, you made it," Jane said, giving her a hug. She figured since Louise was going to be pissed off about the hair, she might as well compound it by bringing her favorite poet. Tonight was going to be perfectly exhilarating. She could feel it.

"Jane, you've made things rather sticky with that hairdo."

"Sorry, sis, but I had no other option. It was a move for solidarity."

"Well, Adrienne, at least you still have hair," Fiona said, their eyes meeting longer than necessary.

Fiona saw Jane catch their lingering exchange and looked slightly puzzled, but Jane didn't know about them having coffee together.

Fiona hadn't stopped thinking about coffee with Adrienne since it happened. The only person she'd told was Margo, who thought it lovely, but then Margo hated Louise.

"She sounds like a free spirit, which is something you need in your life, god knows. Live a little, Fiona. Have a secret friend. It'll be lovely," Margo said, as they sat having lunch on the piazza.

Fiona played with her noodles.

"You should eat. You're looking a little anorectic these days. How many pounds this time?"

"Five or so."

"More like ten," Margo reprimanded. When they finished their meal, she ordered them Italian ice cream.

"I'll get you fat," Margo teased.

"I don't know if this is such a good thing, Margo. I don't know why I didn't say anything about going for coffee," Fiona responded, absently handing the waitress her plate.

The waitress couldn't keep her eyes off Fiona, Margo noticed. How Fiona stayed faithful to Louise all this time was beyond her. Women tripped over themselves when Fiona was around. And Margo wasn't chopped liver, either. At thirty-nine, her auburn hair, pale blue eyes, and lanky frame were nothing to hoot at, but it was Fiona who got the looks.

"To Louise?" Margo asked, trying to keep pace with Fiona's scattered confession.

"Yes. I feel guilty now, and all I did was have coffee."

"And lust in your heart for another woman," Margo teased.

"I did not."

"You did, Fiona. Admit it. You find Adrienne attractive and intriguing, otherwise you wouldn't be stewing over something as mundane as coffee."

"You're right. I do find her intriguing. She is shy

but burning with an intensity, like if you touched her just right some sort of spontaneous combustion would occur. It was strange. And sometimes she'd look at me, and I felt she was staring through."

"Obvious sexual tension," Margo ascertained.

"But she's young. She's Jane's age."

"Oh my god, practically a teenager. In case you've forgotten, Fiona, as you've gotten older so has Jane. That group may act like teenagers, but they're pushing thirty. Time to find the right girlfriend, the one you build your little nest with."

"It certainly wouldn't be with me. I already have that."

"And you're bored with it. Feeling stifled. Tired of the same old, same old," Margo said.

"I could never leave Louise," Fiona said firmly.

"But you have thought about it? Entertained a few fantasies about what it might be like to play around a bit? It's perfectly normal, Fiona. All good people have done it from time to time. It doesn't make you less human, less perfect."

"That's just it. I'm sick of being or trying to be perfect. I want to be me for a while without goals, aspirations, protocol, or rhetoric," Fiona whined.

"You are stifled. Perhaps a few more coffee dates with your new friend might alleviate some of your pent-up anxieties."

"She's coming with Jane for dinner next Thursday," Fiona said.

"Lovely, and you can't wait, right?"

Fiona smiled.

* * * * *

Bel and Jane went to find a book in Fiona's study, looking for some line of a poem they couldn't remember. Fiona and Adrienne stood alone.

"How are you?" Fiona asked gently.

"I'm okay. How about you?"

"I've spent a lot of time thinking about our coffee. I was wondering if you weren't busy, maybe we could have lunch or something?" Fiona asked.

"I'd love to. I'll give you my number and you can call."

"Sounds wonderful," Fiona said.

"See, here it is. I told you it was Rich and not Audre Lorde," Jane said, coming back into the room with Bel close behind her.

"But it sounds like something that Rich would write," Bel replied, diving back into the text greedily.

"Bel, would you like to borrow the book?" Fiona asked.

Bel smiled.

"Please take it," Fiona said, pressing it into her hands.

"Thank you."

"Anything for an aspiring poet," Fiona replied.

"Read us something," Adrienne asked.

Louise answered the door, as everyone else had miraculously disappeared from view. She didn't hold the rest of the heathens accountable, but she was less than pleased with Fiona's lack of protocol. Anne Beaumont was an old college friend of Louise's from her days at Bryn Mawr. Anne had changed a lot since their college years. She was no longer the shy bookworm sequestering herself between stacks of books and reading her way through the world. Lately she had her hands in everything, stirring up trouble with the wave of her lithe arm and causing someone as imperturbable as Benton Peugh, the leader of the conservative right-wingers, to stand up and take notice. Louise was proud of her friend.

Louise had invited the Dyke Defenders to dinner for the express purpose of meeting Anne Beaumont. Her motives were twofold: she didn't want Anne to think she had grown stodgy, and she wanted to be instrumental in bridging the rift between the theorists and the direct action groups. Tonight had the potential to be the crowning moment of her entertaining career.

Entertaining was more than food; it was about making history, and this was Louise's first attempt. She hoped for success. She craved the salons of old where the intellectuals gathered around their stunning hostess and made momentous decisions. Louise was certain she was in a position to do this. Her Internet friend, Kimberly, had given her the idea, and now she was ready. She prayed Jane wouldn't do anything horrid to sabotage her efforts. Louise crossed her fingers and answered the door.

"Louise, you look absolutely radiant," Anne said, looking equally stunning.

"Darling, you haven't changed. Grown more stylish, perhaps."

"I think that stems from having more disposable funds," Anne replied, smoothing down the front of her Saks Fifth Avenue black brocade vest.

Jane was peeking around the den doorway.

"I'll say," Jane muttered to Adrienne, who was supposed to be spying on the star dinner guest but instead had her sights set on Fiona making cocktails in the kitchen.

"I saw that in a catalog. Goes for two-fifty, at least. That's disgusting, if you ask me. Women starving on the streets, scraping up change for Pampers, and she dresses in riches. I can't stand women like that. Where's their sense of social decency?" Jane said, turning to Adrienne. "You're not listening," she admonished.

"Huh?" Adrienne said.

"If I didn't know better, I'd say you were smitten with my sister," Jane said, following Adrienne's line of visual travel.

"Yeah, right, the unobtainable. You must be joking."

"She's beautiful. Who wouldn't look? I'll cut you some slack . . . this time."

"I'll tell you, this group makes me feel downright homely," Bel said, peeking around the door.

"And who might these inquiring young women be?" Anne said, catching the three of them staring.

Fiona came out with the tray of cocktails.

Louise blushed, thinking the girls were cretins for not behaving better. She introduced them. Anne took each of their hands and measured their gaze as if testing their will and fire. She could tell already that Jane was the fiercest.

Louise took Anne's jacket and purse and gave her a tour of the house while Fiona got the rest drinks and led them out onto the back deck. After the tour Anne chatted with Louise while she put the final touches on dinner. Louise did her best to keep things under control through dinner. Food and wine mellowed the group, and Louise began to breathe easier, thinking, perhaps, her plan for finding common ground for these two mutually exclusive camps of lesbian politics might work, that all it took was a civilized dining experience. She was basking in the near attainment of her goal when Anne quizzed Bel about her poetry. Anne had by this time worked her way around the dinner table, probing each woman's secret goals and aspirations.

"What are some of your major poetic themes?"

"Cunts," Bel said bluntly.

Louise blanched. Adrienne looked over at Fiona, who smiled, knowing this was the beginning of the end. Fiona could feel the ball of yarn unraveling across the cosmos. Louise's neat little universe was about to become extremely untidy.

"Interesting choice of subject matter," Anne replied, totally undaunted.

"I firmly believe the way to a woman's heart is through her cunt," Bel continued.

Louise cleared her throat and poured herself another glass of wine.

"But, of course, one should always properly introduce oneself to a vagina first before fully embarking into the lush land of pink vulvas," Anne replied.

Jane raised an eyebrow, obviously impressed. Maybe there was something to this woman beyond tasteful clothing and her bad attitude toward the camp and kitsch of lesbians.

"I'm not as proper as you might think, Jane," Anne said.

Jane was taken aback but quickly recovered. "Perhaps it's just your media image that gives us the impression of a proper Southern belle, minus the accent, bent on placating the masses."

"Is that what you think of what I'm trying to do?"

"If the shoe fits . . ."

"Jane!" Louise said, regaining her composure.

"What are you trying to do?" Bel asked.

"Improve our image, increase our foothold within the political machine, access the average American psyche with something palatable, thus changing their focus from one of abomination to one of tolerance of or social benevolence for cultural difference," Anne replied.

"In other words, sell us out to a world that is capable only of hate," Jane said, glaring at what she now knew for certain to be the enemy.

"Dream world," Bel said shaking her head. "It'll never happen. We tried that before, and we always end up on the short end of the stick."

"If we're not beaten to a pulp with that same stick," Adrienne replied.

Louise opened another bottle of wine.

"Ladies, with the right action, acquiescence is possible," Anne said.

"No, what you're striving for is amalgamation. I refuse to be what the general culture wants. I categorically, ethically, and politically refuse to behave and conform. I refuse to operate under a system that practices intolerance, rape, genocide, and stratification through unfair practices of financial allocations," Jane said, pounding her fist on the table.

Anne smiled, clearly amused. Louise had forgotten Anne's passion for debate. Fiona hadn't forgotten, but she was busy studying Adrienne's profile and thinking about their future lunch date.

Anne began her counterattack. "What I don't understand with your group is this passion for the right-to-lifers. You're lesbians. Why do you care if straight women can't get abortions? Lesbians choose motherhood freely, not out of obligation. Why waste your energies on such a clearly straight focus?"

"Rights cannot be designated according to a woman's sexual orientation. If we let them chisel away at our right to control our own bodies, we allow them into the center of our being. First it will be abortion, then gay and lesbian rights. They think people choose unwanted babies and homosexuality, and by using the rhetoric of choice they turn consequence into a lack of good judgment. Consequently, they also define what is good judgment," Jane retorted.

"Story of our lives . . ." Bel said, sadly shaking her head.

"We fight wherever they start to chisel away at basic human rights, wherever the political machine decides to step in and decide how you live your life. Men want to turn woman's function back to procreation and thus remove her from the public sphere. It's hard to start a revolution with nine infants strapped to your back. By goddess, Atlas couldn't do it. How can women dependent on men, busied to the point of spiritual, physical, and mental exhaustion for having to care for so many mouths, engage in the fight for equal rights? Women are thus rendered totally impotent. Dammit, think for a minute! Women have gained some strategic footholds. Men are worried. *Roe versus Wade* has been with us for some time, but it's only lately that men have focused on the issue. They convince women it's wrong, harness the opposition from the inside, and pivot the issue away from equal rights. The right-to-lifer's purpose isn't to save lives; rather it is to capture and control!" Jane was standing.

Anne was impressed with her passion. She was moved, something that didn't happen often. She had crossed the Dyke Defenders off as nothing more than a nuisance. Her encounter with Jane was changing her mind. It would take some doing, but perhaps she could overcome her distaste of direct action groups if it meant getting involved with someone like Jane. This could prove to be amusing, and she was in the mood for some diversion. Jane looked like she might prove an interesting one.

"Shall we have dessert?" Louise asked weakly and left for the kitchen.

"Why, yes, and then I'll read us an inspirational poem," Bel said, smiling big. She was happy to have a good meal and interesting company.

Jane sat down. "No rebuttal?" she asked.

"Hmm, thinking," Anne replied, returning Jane's gaze.

Louise returned with a chocolate mousse, hoping food would distract. It worked. Anne pondered Jane's philosophy while they reminisced about college days, telling their younger cohorts of earlier days of women, love, and academic pitfalls. Louise considered her dinner party a complete disaster, and listening to cunt poetry put her over the edge. The girls would be gone soon and the hideous thing over. Louise tried to relax and bide her time.

* * * * *

"Where are you two off to in such a hurry?" Anne asked, watching with interest as Jane quickly changed from appropriate dinner wear to her standard grunge in the middle of the kitchen.

"Jane, believe it or not, this house has several other rooms. You could use one of them to change. The kitchen is hardly the place for it," Louise said.

"Yeah, yeah. We're all women here. I'm sure you've seen it before," Jane replied. "We're going to a Rave at First Ave. Great place to recruit dykes. We're doing posters and handouts for next month's meeting."

"Sounds productive and fun," Anne said amiably.

Jane eyed Anne suspiciously, thinking this is where the older, more serious feminists would insert the *but* clause and start in on being responsible, like Shouldn't you be doing something more constructive, expending your energies in more serious directions? The *but* clause never came.

"I'd like to sit in on one of your meetings. Interview a few of the women for my next book," Anne said.

"We don't do books," Jane replied.

"Why not?"

"Because that would make us groovy, and lesbians would join only to be part of the celebrity stuff. It reduces the movement to pure trendiness," Jane replied.

"Think about it. Maybe you'll change your mind," Anne said.

"I doubt it."

* * * * *

Jane threw the car in reverse and skidded out of the driveway.

"Jane, why do you think lesbians really join the movement?" Adrienne asked, lighting Jane a cigarette and taking a few perfunctory drags for the high feeling it gave her.

"I don't know. What do you think?"

"To get laid," Adrienne replied.

"No!"

"That's why I joined. I wanted to meet interesting women and find someone to fuck."

"You're a superficial excuse for a lesbian."

"Jane!"

"I'm kidding. Shit, why do you think I started the group?"

"I would have thought for political reasons," Adrienne said.

"Wrong. To get laid."

"Seriously?" Adrienne asked incredulously.

"Seriously. Beats the bar, doesn't it?"

"You mean to tell me this amazing political feat is based on women getting laid?" Adrienne said.

"Yep. Who said only men think with their little heads."

"Great. Lesbians think with their hormones," Adrienne said.

"Beautiful, isn't it? All basic human functions evolve around having an orgasm. That's why it's hard to trust a straight woman. She doesn't have them. We can only come together if we all have the same mystical experience of coming."

"Don't let Anne Beaumont find out. She'd be thoroughly disgusted," Adrienne advised.

"Who gives a fuck. I can't stand women like that,

and I certainly don't want her anywhere near the Defenders. I won't have her turn us into another one of her dissertations on the history of the feminist movement. We're not about that. We're fluid and changing too quickly to be defined and discussed in some chapter by someone who wants everybody pigeonholed to fit her definitions. I refuse."

"Maybe you're right," Adrienne said.

"Of course I'm right. Oh my god I sound just like Louise. We've got to stop going there. She's rubbing off."

Adrienne laughed. "You'll probably grow up to be just like her."

"Never. Shoot me if I do."

"Deal."

Jane looked in the rearview mirror to make sure Bel and Claudette were still behind them. She'd forgotten in her rant about Anne Beaumont that she was supposed to be leading them from the obscure back streets where Fiona lived into the downtown area. She smiled. Bel was right on her ass.

"And where are you off to?" Margo said, sauntering into Fiona's office.

"Lunch."

"At ten-thirty in the morning?" Margo said, checking her watch.

"I've got some errands to run," Fiona said, frantically searching for her Day-Timer.

"Perhaps I could meet you for lunch at a more suitable hour, say noon."

"Well . . ."

Margo put her forefinger to her pursed lips. "Oh, I get it. You're having lunch with someone. Might I hazard a guess? Cute and young, with strange hair."

Fiona blushed.

"Guessed right. Evil lady. What would your wife say? Trouble, trouble, trouble. I wonder what Adrienne looks like with a full head of hair? Perfectly darling, I'm sure. Well, I won't detain you. Have fun and don't do anything I wouldn't do," Margo said, leaving.

Fiona stood, holding her Day-Timer and feeling rattled. What was she doing? Was it evil? Lunch. I'm having lunch, that's what I'm doing. Having lunch is not having an affair. Would she tell Louise if she asked? Fiona scanned her list of errands. No. Why should she? Because Louise wouldn't like it, she wouldn't understand it, and she'd be jealous. There, I said it, Fiona told her conscience. She wanted to buy Adrienne the book she'd expressed interest in last time they were together. A book of photographs by Judy Francesco.

The restaurant was crowded when Fiona arrived. Adrienne saved a table. She smiled shyly as Fiona approached.

"You look nice," Fiona said, noticing the well-tailored shirt.

"I borrowed it from Jane. One of the dinner shirts. She appears to have quite the collection. I told her I was going for a job interview," Adrienne said.

"I see," Fiona said slowly.

"I wasn't sure you'd like her knowing we were having lunch."

"It wouldn't matter, really," Fiona said.

"Wouldn't it?" Adrienne said, staring straight at her.

"Louise doesn't know," Fiona said, playing with her silverware.

"I didn't think she did," Adrienne said.

"Now we know where we stand."

"Yes."

"I brought you a present," Fiona said, handing her the book.

Adrienne blushed. "Thank you."

"I thought it might help you with your photography."

"And as Jane would say, you could always masturbate to the pictures if all else fails."

"Yes," Fiona said laughing. The tension was broken, and now they could have a nice lunch.

"Shall we raid the salad bar?" Fiona asked.

"Please. I'm famished," Adrienne replied.

"I like a woman with an appetite," Fiona teased.

Adrienne smiled.

Fiona neatly placed her items from the salad bar on her plate while Adrienne placed extra items on top.

"But what if I don't like those?"

"You can take them off."

Fiona gently bumped her hip against Adrienne's. "If I didn't know better, I'd say you were being a brat."

"I would never," Adrienne said, dumping a wad of grated carrots on Fiona's plate.

"I draw the line at carrots," Fiona said.

"Good roughage."

"My bowels are fine, thank you."

"We must be getting intimate," Adrienne said.

"I'd like that."

"Me too," Adrienne said, removing the carrots.

They sat down. Adrienne mentally cataloged everything Fiona had on her plate. Those were the things she liked.

"What did you think of the dinner party?" Fiona asked.

"It was interesting. But I do have a confession to make."

"Yes?"

"Watching Louise, as decorum fell by the wayside, was my favorite part. Then I felt bad afterward, because it must have been very unpleasant for her."

"I have a confession also. I secretly enjoyed those moments too. Don't feel bad. I'm the heinous bitch who should have more respect and empathy for the situation. It's just that for all her planning, she can't plan people. And she shouldn't want to. She wasn't always like this. Somewhere along the line something happened."

"Was she mad?"

"Not too angry. She was better in the morning," Fiona replied, thinking about how they had both gone to bed hurt and angry. Louise had been convinced the dinner was a complete disaster. Fiona had tried to comfort her, but Louise pushed her away. Fiona had lain awake thinking, I can't take much more of this. The next morning she got up early and went running, trying to clear her head. Louise was civil to her when she got back. Fiona was tired of civil. She wanted to scream. Hate me or love me, but please stop hurting me this way.

"So you got everything patched up by morning?"

"Oh yes. It was fine."

"I was kind of worried. I love Jane, but sometimes she makes things difficult," Adrienne said, wishing she had the courage to take Fiona's hand and say, If you ever need someone to talk to, someone to hold you when you're sad, I'm here. But she knew that would be presumptuous. Fiona was too private to reveal her pains and anguish to anyone, much less a virtual stranger.

"Now tell me one of your deep dark secrets," Fiona asked.

"So many. Let me think. Oh my god, there's a stray piece of carrot on your plate. An oversight."

Their hands touched briefly as Adrienne neatly extracted the carrot. Fiona darted back like her touch was full of fire.

"I'm sorry," Adrienne said.

"No. It just surprised me."

Their eyes met.

"You have lovely eyes, Adrienne."

"Thank you. And you have the most incredible legs I've ever seen."

"Thanks. It's been a long time since someone told me that."

"You should be told that daily," Adrienne said.

"Perhaps that could be your new job."

"Gladly," Adrienne said, wishing she'd put more stuff on her plate so lunch would last longer.

Five

Sarah and Mary were laughing hysterically when Jane came into the office.

"What's so funny?" Jane asked, skating back behind the two of them as they sat huddled in front of Mary's Macintosh.

"Look at what we've done," Sarah said, beaming with pride.

"Is that who I think it is?" Jane said, peering at the photo image on the screen.

"If you mean Benton Peugh, you are correct," Mary replied.

"He looks different."

"Like a bad drag queen?" Sarah said.

They broke into laughter.

"Exactly," Jane replied.

"The wonders of modern technology, a scanner, and an art program go a long way," Mary said, obviously pleased with her efforts.

"This is awesome. Print me a copy," Jane said.

Jane took the copy, taped it to the wall, and proceeded to throw darts at it.

"Feel better?" Mary asked.

"Much."

"I know we were just playing around with this, but perhaps we could put this to a greater use," Sarah said.

"Meaning?" Jane asked, wondering what stupid idea Stupid Girl would come up with this time.

"I think we should send this to one of those sleazy tabloid magazines and see if they take it. It could be an exclusive. Benton Peugh's secret life as a drag queen. It would make a great cover," Sarah replied.

Jane stopped skating around the room. "That is a perfectly brilliant idea. You know, Mary, I was wrong. There is furniture in there, and maybe even a lamp or two."

She took Sarah by the shoulders and stared into her eyes.

"Yes, I'm sure of it. We might have to purchase a few lightbulbs, but there is hope."

Sarah looked at Mary for help.

"What is she talking about?" Sarah asked.

"Nothing, but she's right. Your idea is brilliant. They probably won't take it to print, but it's worth a try."

"I have something else that might interest you," Mary said, handing Jane the agenda of Benton Peugh's tour of Minneapolis.

"I like this part, especially the address of where he's staying. Perhaps he'll have us in for tea," Sarah said flippantly.

"I doubt that, but we can certainly make a ruckus outside the hotel, which will certainly draw some media attention. And you know how we like attention," Jane said, doing a pirouette in the center of the room.

Adrienne came in sporting a camera. She went right up to Jane and snapped a closeup.

"New toy?" Jane asked.

"Hmm."

"Purpose?" Jane asked.

"It's high time the Dyke Defenders start being documented. I intend to take the position of photographer, and I was hoping Mary, with those massive brain cells of hers, might supply brilliant text," Adrienne said.

"Is this your way of serving posterity without Anne Beaumont?" Jane asked.

"You got it."

"Speaking of her, she's called every day, sometimes twice, and her e-mail is becoming a distraction. Call her, write her, anything. I'm sure she thinks I'm not giving you her messages. She's not someone to mess with, Jane," Mary said.

"Why haven't you called her?" Adrienne asked, snapping another photo. Jane skated across the room and leapt up on the back of the couch, which made a precarious creaking noise.

"Yes, why haven't you called me?" Anne asked, from the doorway.

"Incredible timing. You're not spying on us, are you?" Jane asked, still balancing on the back of the couch.

"No, but I do have good timing. Didn't your mother tell you not to skate on the furniture when you were a child?"

"She taught me how," Jane retorted.

"So why haven't you returned my calls?"

"I don't see the point."

"How do you know what the point is if you don't try?" Anne said, undaunted.

"We come from totally opposite camps. You don't like our politics, and we think yours suck. What's the point?"

"We might not be at such odds as you think. Come to coffee, please."

"What do you want from me?" Jane asked.

"Jane, try to be civil," Adrienne warned.

"I want to talk to you. Find out what goes on here. That's all. Certainly you don't begrudge me a half hour."

"Jane, go," Adrienne said.

"I won't call any more if you'll come for coffee," Anne said.

"You promise?" Jane said.

"I promise. Unless you instruct me otherwise."

"I doubt that," Jane said, doing a cartwheel off the couch.

They left. Jane looked like a truant heading off with the dean of students. Anne reminded Jane of her less-than-pleasant schooldays.

"Why does Jane have such an aversion to that woman? She might be extremely useful some day," Mary said.

"Beaumont is an authority figure. Jane hates authority," Adrienne replied. She didn't quite understand the interest that the grande dame of political theory had in Jane either, but she couldn't reduce it to pure lust, although that was the vibe she was getting. She tried to envision Anne Beaumont with the hots for Jane. But she quickly dismissed the idea as ludicrous. Beaumont was too much of a cold fish for something like lust to rule any of her behaviors.

"Why do you hate me?" Anne asked as she dumped three containers of half-and-half in her large coffee.

Jane looked up at her with lips covered in the froth of her cappuccino and chocolate sprinkles.

Anne laughed. "Do you always cover your face in cream like that?" she said.

"It's good for the complexion. I don't hate you. I don't think about you," Jane said.

"You have got to be the bluntest woman I have ever known."

"Is that why you're interested?" Jane said.

"Probably. If you were more taciturn I wouldn't bother. You say exactly what's on your mind, and I like that," Anne said.

"Are you missing that particular attribute with the group you're hanging with and that's why you're interested in ours?"

Anne sipped her coffee and studied Jane. "You're being rather protective of your brainchild. Slightly paranoid you might be losing control?"

"Fuck you," Jane said, getting up and leaving.

Anne was stunned. Jane was gone before she had time to think.

"You're back in a hurry," Adrienne said.

"Shortest coffee on record," Jane replied.

"What happened?" Mary asked.

"The woman's a dick, and I don't have time for her shit."

"She didn't proposition you, did she?" Adrienne said.

"God no. I don't think she'd go to this much trouble just to get laid."

"What is she about then?" Adrienne asked.

"I don't know. But I don't think she's going to give up. So what do we do when faced with an adversary? Girls?" Jane said.

"Research," Mary replied.

"Exactly," Jane said, patting Mary on the back.

"Why do you consider her an adversary?" Adrienne asked.

"Is she on our side?" Jane queried.

"I don't know," Adrienne said.

"We consider her an adversary until proven otherwise."

"Us, them, us, them," Adrienne said, smiling at Jane.

"Yep. Okay, women, let's get to work. Adrienne, come with me. I want to scope out the hotel where Benton is staying."

"Sarah, would you like to come to the library with me to do some homework on Beaumont?" Mary asked, trying not to blush for being forward. She expected to be turned down. She straightened her shoulders in the anticipation of being let down. Women like Sarah didn't go to the library with homely women like herself.

"I'd love to," Sarah said, beaming.

Mary's face dropped despite her best intentions at being composed.

Jane winked at Mary and grabbed her crotch.

Mary blanched and silently thanked God that Sarah's back was turned and she missed the whole thing.

"If I didn't know better, I'd think Sarah is falling in love with Mary," Jane said over her shoulder as she headed toward the street.

"You think so?" Adrienne said, having never considered the possibility before.

"Watch them next time they're together."

"You have antennae for stuff like that."

"Love radar," Jane said.

Adrienne instantly felt better. Not all intuitions were correct. There was always a margin of error. Jane would know if Anne had the hots for her. Adrienne didn't know why their afternoon interlude made her nervous, but she had a bad feeling, like the foreshadowing of a plague, about Anne Beaumont coming into their lives. Maybe that was Beaumont's agenda. Infiltrate and destroy.

Adrienne heaved the last box from the freight elevator.

"I'm done with this moving shit!" Jane muttered.

"You're the asshole who bought the building," Adrienne said.

"Don't remind me. It was not, however, my idea," Jane replied, looking over at Fiona, who was sitting on a box and guzzling bottled water.

"It'll be wonderful in the end," Fiona promised. Wonderful and frightening. It seemed lately that the wonder in her life also had the underside of fright: Two entirely different emotions suddenly wrapped around one another like a spiral, separate yet linked. Whenever she thought about Adrienne, she experienced vertigo as she felt herself climbing up the spiral. And now she was going to be even closer to Adrienne. Her office was on the top floor, Adrienne's loft apartment was just below, Bel lived next door, and Jane and Claudette were four doors down. There was still room for three more occupants.

"Are you sure all this togetherness isn't going to kill us?" Jane asked.

"Do you spend all your time together now?" Fiona asked.

"Yes."

"Then you answered your own question. Think of it as saving transportation costs and lessening global pollution," Fiona said, smiling at Adrienne. Mention saving the environment, and Jane could be convinced of anything.

"Hmm . . . I guess you're right," Jane said.

Adrienne smiled back and took the proffered bottle of water. Her lips touched where Fiona's had. Infatuation is a dangerous thing, a sick thing, pure insanity, so why do we entertain it, crave it, create it? It's ethereal. And ethereal things never last, Adrienne told herself. Perhaps being close to Fiona would decrease her craving. They would have togetherness and yet space. They could become friends and then never think twice about crossing boundaries. Adrienne knew she was lying to herself.

All she wanted was to see, to be near, to talk to, and to touch Fiona. Fiona was all she thought of. She'd already read every story she could find on unrequited love through the history of humankind, and it still didn't stop the craving or make her understand it any better. All she learned was that unrequited love became consummated and then inevitably ended in various forms of personal disaster. The story of Isolde and Tristan was her favorite because it was the most sensuous. Adrienne was a sucker for sensuousness. She knew Fiona was sensuous, and like a bloodhound on the trail, she followed, knowing full well her prey would sting when captured. But she was undaunted nonetheless.

"Fiona, are you coming to Friday night's demonstration?" Jane asked.

Fiona smiled and shook her head.

"She never comes, but I always like to ask," Jane told Adrienne.

"I'll come sometime," Fiona said.

"Come Friday then," Jane said.

"I can't. Dinner party. But I will come some other night."

"Yeah, I'll believe that when I see it. Well, catch us on the news at least."

"Of course. I wouldn't miss it," Fiona replied, thinking how much it irritated Louise, but she did it anyway. No amount of disapproval could daunt her pride in Jane.

"Since you're booked for Friday, how about finishing off tonight with pizza at Slice of New York and then shaking a few legs at the First Ave? Killer band tonight."

"I don't know, Jane. I should probably get home..." Fiona replied, looking mildly persuadable.

Jane leaped. "Call. Consider it girls' night out. When was the last time?"

Fiona's face registered a blank.

"Forever," Jane said.

Jane dialed the number and handed the phone to Fiona, who discreetly walked into the other room.

Jane looked at Adrienne. "She's so well mannered."

"What the fuck happened to you?"

Jane threw a couch pillow at her. "I resent that. I have manners. They're well hidden beneath a hardened exterior built for survival on the streets."

"You're full of shit," Adrienne said.

"Thank you. Now let's have beer. Shall we see if we can get Sis trashed tonight?"

"That would be interesting."

"Let's start her early," Jane said, taking Fiona a cold one.

Louise wasn't happy. Fiona could tell by the tone of her voice.

"I'll be home early. I promise."

"I knew your moving into that building was going to create problems. Now you'll be associating with those hoodlums on a daily basis," Louise said.

"Are you calling my sister a hoodlum?"

"She certainly acts like one and has a police record to back it up."

"They're for political reasons," Fiona said.

"Look, I don't want to get into this now," Louise said.

"Why are you angry?"

"I'm not," Louise said.

"It's not like I'm out fooling around. I *am* with Jane."

"It's not Jane I'm worried about," Louise said, glancing at the clock on the wall.

"What's that supposed to mean?"

"Nothing. I'll see you later. Be careful."

Fiona took a long swig of beer.

"Let me guess. Louise isn't happy. Well, fuck her. Guzzle that and let's go," Jane commanded.

"Are we late?" Fiona asked.

"Since when have you become time oriented?" Adrienne teased.

"Since I'm famished," Jane said, taking Adrienne and her sister's arm and leading them to the street.

Horace, the young man behind the counter at Slice of New York, beamed the moment they walked in the door.

"Jane, baby, how's it hanging? Oh, sweetie darling who's the dish?"

"Boy, Horace, what about me?" Adrienne said.

"Oh, baby, I know you already," Horace said, smiling wide and dismissing her with a swish of his hand.

"Horace, this is my sister, Fiona."

"Nice to meet you," Horace said, leaning on the counter. "You two don't look like sisters."

"It was the milkman, Horace," Jane said.

"Now why are people always blaming the milkman? My daddy was a milkman and all us children look the same."

"Well then, since Mom's a teacher maybe it was a visiting professor," Jane said.

"Jane!" Fiona said, blushing.

Horace put a hand on his hip and shook his head prophetically. "Honey, I think her daddy was the better looking one."

"She got beauty and I got bravado," Jane said.

"I'll say. Having the usual?" Horace asked.

"Of course, and bring us two pitchers of beer. I feel a powerful thirst coming on," Jane said.

"Where's Claudette?" Fiona asked.

"She'll be here. She'd having a rendezvous with the spy."

"What spy?"

"Benton Peugh's appointment secretary."

"You have an insider?" Fiona asked incredulously.

"Damn right. There are several ways to skin a cat, which I, of course, would never do, being the animal rights activist I am, except for those unpleasant wildlife accidents," Jane said, her conscience troubling her slightly.

"Isn't that rather dishonest?"

"Wake up, Fiona. He's got the world on his side. All we've got is each other. We're just playing the odds. Hang with us and you'll learn all sorts of things," Jane said.

"I'm sure I will," Fiona replied.

"Before the night is over, you'll know all."

"Jane, please don't get me in trouble."

"Sis, you were in trouble the minute you went left instead of right at the door."

"Why do I get the feeling you're correct?" Fiona whined.

"The night is young," Jane said.

Mary found Jane, Claudette, Bel, and Adrienne tumbled in a heap on the king-size futon in the office. The room showed definite signs of a party; cigarettes and beer bottles littered every tabletop.

The phone rang.

"Dyke Defenders. How may I help you?" Mary said.

"I want to speak with that cretin," said the surly voice on the other end.

"Which one?" Mary asked.

"The bald one."

"Jane?"

"You're most astute."

"May I ask who is calling?"

"Tell her it's Martha Stewart."

"One moment."

Mary dragged the phone over to Jane and gently tapped her shoulder. Jane groaned and rolled over. She opened one eye and tried to focus. It looked like Mary, but she wasn't entirely sure.

"Morning, sunshine. Are you taking calls?"

"Depends."

"It's Martha Stewart," Mary said, handing her the phone.

"Hello, darling. Have you already redecorated the house and planned the housewarming party, complete with sculptured radishes?"

"What is the meaning of this?" Louise snarled.

"Meaning of what? Life, liberty, and the pursuit of orgasm. On the latter I'd have to say system of reward for fulfilling a crucial bodily function. What a plan, wouldn't you say?"

"Could you stop being a heinous asshole for just three seconds?" Louise said.

"I like when you talk dirty to me," Jane said, rolling on her side and smiling devilishly at Adrienne, who had just waked up.

"Jane, I'm going to fucking kill you," Louise said, instantly berating herself for losing all sense of decorum.

"There now, we can talk. What's on your mind, sweetheart?"

"Fiona and the state she arrived home in last night and the fact she's puking as we speak. What did you do to her?"

"I didn't do anything. Fiona's a big girl."

"You're a bad influence."

"Thank you."

"It's not a compliment," Louise said.

"That depends on your point of reference."

"I want you and your little heathen friends to stay away from her."

"If you want to fight, Louise, that's fine but remember, blood is thicker than water. You may fuck her, but she's my sister. Come between us and you'll lose," Jane said.

"I wouldn't count on it."

"Louise, go bake something and leave us alone."

"Ugh, you make me so mad."

"Good. Now go away."

Jane handed Myrna the phone.

"Great way to start the day," Jane said, bouncing

up and heading straight for the fridge to get a Dr Pepper.

Claudette and Bel made morning noises, and Adrienne got up.

"Trouble in paradise?" Adrienne asked.

"Yep. Louise is downright pissed, and Fiona is hung over."

"Hey, babycakes," Claudette said, getting up and kissing Jane gently on the forehead before wandering off to the couch with Jane's soda. Jane didn't miss a beat. She opened the fridge and got another soda.

"You guys look like you had a good time last night," Mary said, beginning the trash detail.

"Damn good time. Let's go get breakfast," Jane said.

"Shower first," Adrienne said.

"How do you feel?" Jane asked.

"Not great, but nothing hot water and hashbrowns can't fix," Adrienne replied.

"Now that's the spirit," Jane said.

When Adrienne got out of the shower, Fiona was lying on the couch with a baseball hat pulled over her eyes.

"You puked, huh?" Jane inquired.

"I don't want to talk about it," Fiona grumbled.

"But you had fun, didn't you?" Jane said.

"Yes, but I forgot about the payment. I hate the morning after."

"Are you all right?" Adrienne asked.

Fiona lifted up her cap and smiled at her. "As best as can be expected."

"What state did you arrive in?" Claudette asked.

"I fell asleep in my clothes in the middle of the living room after I made a rather large mess in the kitchen trying to make a sandwich. You-know-who was not happy."

"So what's new?" Jane said.

"Where's Bel?" Adrienne said.

"Work," Claudette said.

"Oh goddess. Not my idea of fun."

"I don't think I'll be getting much of that done myself," Fiona said, pulling the cap over her eyes.

"Good. Then come to breakfast," Jane said.

"Jane, remember, tonight is the demonstration," Mary warned.

"I'll have everyone fixed up in no time. Ladies, let us go feast."

Jane came flying up the stairs. Mary looked up, smiling.

"Obviously feeling better," Mary said.

"Breakfast, a quick scope of Benton's hotel, and I feel great. Hangover successfully overcome."

"Claudette?"

"Getting with her pals at the news station just in case there's a scene," Jane said.

"Adrienne?"

"Taking a stroll with my sister. Go figure that one. And then she's going to get Bel's van so we can load it and then pick her up at work by five."

"I've almost completed the newsletter except for tonight's scene of bravado, and Sarah is becoming a regular at the library finding out stuff about your new pal. Speaking of which, these came for you," Mary said, pointing to the display of yellow roses on the table.

"Mary, you shouldn't have," Jane said, batting her eyelashes.

"I didn't. That Camille Paglia wanna-be did."

"Maybe I should tell people to fuck off more often. I'd get more presents that way. Did I tell you I need a miter saw?"

"You told her to fuck off?" Mary said.

"Yes. She accused me of being paranoid about losing control of the group. I didn't bother to tell her I'm not in control. In an anarchist group there is no place for a CEO."

Jane smelled the roses and then opened the window. She poked her head outside.

"What are you doing?" Mary asked, as Jane picked up the vase of roses and walked to the window.

"What do you think I'm going to do?" Jane said, turning and neatly dropping the roses four flights.

Mary heard the crash of glass.

"I hope you didn't hit anyone."

"I didn't," Jane said.

"Why did you do that?"

"Because the woman is annoying, and a dozen roses is not going to change my opinion. It would be hypocritical to keep them. Don't you agree?"

"Wholeheartedly," Mary said, going back to her computer.

"Do you feel better?" Adrienne asked, looking the picture of concern.

"Much, thank you. I don't think I'll be running today, but a long walk feels good. I'm glad you came along. It made it nice," Fiona said, looking over at Adrienne, who blushed slightly.

"I liked it. Jane reminded me about walking to see, to smell, to think about things. Her Walt Whitman walks."

"Jane, my incorrigible, beautiful sister. What would I do without Jane?"

"Have you two always been close?"

"Not as close as we are now. Coming out like we did has brought us closer together because we have that important thing in common, and it was easier to join forces than to go it alone."

"How did your parents handle two of you?"

"As lesbians?" Fiona asked.

"Yes."

"I don't know that it's so much worse. With two of us, there isn't a natural contrast like there would be if one was straight. The good one who gets married and has the kids versus the bad one who refuses to adhere to the system. This way we're equal."

"True."

"What are your siblings like?"

"I don't have any. I wish I did. I always wanted a sister. Obviously, I'm a rather large letdown in the perfect-daughter department. We talk, but we're not close. My parents live on the West Coast," Adrienne said.

"Have you met our mother yet?"

"No, I haven't had the pleasure."

"You'll have to come for tea. Hazel is a remarkable woman. You'd like her," Fiona said.

"Just say when."

"I will."

They came to the front of the Dyke Defender building. Bel, the sign painter by day, had made them an incredible sign for the outside of the new building. That was how Jane met Bel. She was painting a sign for one of the offbeat galleries downtown. Bel was given full artistic license, and the sign turned out to be beautiful. Jane sat and watched, and when the work was done she had bought Bel a drink. They'd been friends ever since.

"Nice sign," Fiona said, staring up the large red letters with the rainbow border and a fist held sky- ward.

"Bel just finished it," Adrienne said, standing in the middle of broken glass and yellow roses. She bent down and picked up the water-soaked card. It read "Apologies accepted, I hope" and was signed by Anne Beaumont.

Fiona turned around.

"What's this?" Fiona asked.

"They were for Jane from Anne Beaumont," Adrienne said, looking up at the open window with the white sheer fluttering in and out of it like a piece of lung tissue engaged in the act of breathing.

"Why do I get the feeling this wasn't an accident?" Fiona said.

"Because the evidence does not point in that direction," Adrienne said.

"Do you think Anne is enamored with Jane?"

"Stranger things have happened," Adrienne said, looking keenly at Fiona.

"Yes, yes they have."

* * * * *

"Is everyone ready?" Jane asked as the van pulled up in front of the Hyatt Regency.

"I'm scared, Jane. I don't know if I'm ready for this," Sarah said, looking pale and chewing the cuticle of her right forefinger.

"You'll be fine. Everyone is always nervous her first time out. It's like losing your virginity. A fright, then ecstasy, then the flood of undulating accomplishment for having faced your fears. Eleanor Roosevelt once said that you gain strength, confidence, and courage when you face your fears. Sarah, grab your metaphoric balls and come on, honey. We're playing with the big boys now," Jane said, pushing her out of the van.

"It'll be all right, sweetheart. I remember my first time. Damn, I got so nervous I puked. Ask Jane," Bel said.

"I think it may have been nerves, but I think the pint of Jack Daniel's you drank had something to do with it too."

"I'm sure it did. Hey, Mary, did you bring the cans of Lysol?" Bel said.

"Of course. Here're the lighters too," Mary said, tossing a can in Sarah's direction.

"This is a killer idea," Claudette said, turning away from them and testing out her newly learned art of fire throwing.

"You can thank Sarah for it," Mary said, trying not to beam with pride.

Claudette raised an eyebrow in Jane's direction, and Jane nodded.

"This is awesome!" Claudette said, sending a spray of fire into the atmosphere.

"I'm not so sure the environmental groups will see it that way," Adrienne said, taking a photograph of Claudette in action.

"What's this?" Claudette inquired.

"Photodocumentation. An important aspect of any movement," Adrienne said. "Since Jane won't let us have Anne Beaumont do a piece on us, I felt it my duty to at least start the process. We have been grossly negligent in recording our history."

"Shit!" Sarah screamed.

"What?" Jane asked.

"Nothing," Sarah said, putting her hand behind her back.

"Let me guess. You burned yourself," Jane said, pulling on Sarah's arm.

The damaged hand was brought forth. The group examined it.

"This is not good," Claudette said, looking at the bright red appendage.

Adrienne was snapping pictures.

"Will you stop that. This is no time for a photo session," Jane said.

"You can't screen documentation because something unpleasant happens," Adrienne said, taking a photo of Jane scowling at her.

"I can see your new hobby is going to prove troublesome," Jane said.

"It's not a hobby. This is important work. Don't belittle it. Just because you live entirely in the moment doesn't mean the past isn't important. We owe it to the children," Adrienne said.

"What children?" Jane said.

"The lesbians born and not yet born," Adrienne said.

"What shit have you been reading? I never took you for one who reads feminist propaganda," Jane said.

"Fuck you," Adrienne said.

"Ladies, come on. Now is not the time," Claudette said.

"Here, Sarah, put this on it," Mary said, handing her a small plastic bag filled with ice.

"Where'd you get that?" Jane asked.

"We're at a hotel, remember? There's an ice machine on every floor," Mary said.

"Right."

"Jane, I want you to apologize to Adrienne. You're wrong to call her work a hobby. That's typical patriarchal language," Claudette said.

Jane pursed her lips.

"All right, I'm sorry. It's stress and I have my period. It's hard to be congenial when you're bleeding profusely. An activist does not have time for banal bodily functions."

"Menstruation is not banal. It's a beautiful part of our femaleness," Sarah said.

"Fuck! I can't say anything right," Jane said.

"Are you sure you're supposed to put ice on a burn?" Bel asked, examining Sarah's hand.

"How the fuck do I know? Do I look like a doctor?" Jane said, reaching a maximum level of irritation. She rubbed her temples.

"Someone really should take a course in first aid," Mary said, putting that on her immense mental to-do list. "Bel, perhaps we should draft you to take a course. You seem very levelheaded in a crisis situation," she added. "I'll research it."

"Sure. I could do that," Bel said.

"Do you think we could have this discussion another time? We do have a demonstration to put on," Jane said, watching the long black limo with the license plate *LIFE* on it pull up front.

The chauffeur opened the door for Benton Peugh and winked at Claudette. The spy had done her job, and the girls were now in place.

"How is it that those horrendous women, or rather lesbians, always seem to know just where I'll be? They get as much press as I do. I'm not happy about it. I shall have to have Susan look into that," Benton Peugh said.

"Yes, sir."

"Why don't they grow up and become real women, wives and mothers, instead of social deviants parading around creating havoc wherever they go? It's perfectly disgusting."

The chauffeur nodded. She was used to Benton's tirades, his series of rhetorical questions to which he did not want answers. She had learned to nod accordingly while secretly slipping the Defenders his travel plans. It was her retribution. It was the reason she drove his fat, white, bigoted ass around.

The news cameras showed up while the Defenders screamed chants.

"Two, four, six, eight, love not hate!" the women screamed as Benton Peugh rushed past, obviously perturbed at being accosted again.

"Two, four, six, eight, sit on my face!" Sarah screeched.

The cameras turned to catch her being nudged by Mary, who whispered, "Love not hate."

"Can't you get it right?" Jane admonished, looking as perturbed as Benton Peugh.

"I get stage fright," Sarah replied.

"Two, four, six, eight, hey, Benton, want a date, can't be late," Bel screeched, laughing hysterically.

Benton Peugh turned and scowled. It was the perfect moment to start the flame-throwing spectacle with Adrienne and Claudette leading the pack. Benton Peugh jumped back, and the photographers aptly captured his look of disdain, then alarm. Great morning-papers material, Adrienne thought.

With Benton Peugh and his entourage safely inside, the Defenders continued the flame throwing and chanting, trying to make as much ruckus as possible, flashing signs, and banging on garbage-can lids. People stopped on the street to gawk. Some offered encouragement, while others hurled insults that were hurled back with equal precision. Jane's face was flushed with happiness. This was her favorite part of direct action, the confrontation. The television crew began to pack up.

"The only problem with our system is that it's all so short-lived," Jane said. "Somehow we need to prolong it."

"Sounds a bit like orgasm — something strived for but much too short. The trials and tribulations of protest," Claudette said.

"Why don't we go inside?" Adrienne said. "It is a free country, and we do pay taxes."

"Yeah, taxes for rights we don't have," Jane grumbled.

"Let's go," Bel said, locking up the van.

There was no discussion. Each looked at the other,

nodding heads in agreement, and they stormed the Hyatt. The television crew, smelling additional coverage, turned around and took up the rear.

"No flame throwing," Jane told Bel.

"All right," Bel said, tucking the can of Lysol in her back pocket. So much for the grand lobby spectacle she had envisioned. Jane was right. It was too dangerous. She could see the headlines now, DEFENDERS TORCH HYATT, which would be fine if it was intentional, but with their luck it would be accidental, something like Sarah setting a curtain on fire. Bel took the can away from Sarah as a precaution.

They bustled through the lobby.

Jane turned in panic to Mary. "What room is he in?"

"Three-fourteen," Mary said, pushing the button for the elevator.

"What would I do without you?" Jane asked.

"Be less organized," Mary replied.

They started making their ruckus the minute they got out of the elevator. All the way down the hallway they announced their arrival.

Benton's aide came out, anticipating the worst. He was not disappointed.

"Now, young ladies, I don't know what you think you're doing, but this is not the place. Mr. Peugh is a very busy man and he doesn't have time for such nonsense."

"Protest is the only way we get anything done in this country. Historically —" Jane started in.

"Yes, yes. Well that's all fine, but —" the aide said.

"But what?" Jane said, cutting him off.

"Harold, what's going on out there?" Benton said, coming to the door.

"Nothing, sir. I've got it all under control."

Jane gave the signal, and the noise started in.

"That doesn't appear to the case," Benton said, stepping out into the hall.

The camera crew scrambled up just in time to catch Benton looking momentarily bewildered. He quickly regained his composure.

"I really think you should explain yourselves. You are committing an act of invasion. Surely a man is entitled to some privacy," Benton said.

"What you do with your lawmaking is an invasion on our bodies. Where is our privacy as you make our wombs your public, trying to make them your property," Jane said, pointing a defiant finger at Benton.

"Sarah, what are you doing here? You can't possibly be connected with these women."

Jane turned to look at Sarah. "You know him?"

Benton answered for her, "Why, I've known her since she was just a little girl. Sweetest little thing you ever saw. Pride of her daddy's eye. But Sarah, this? Does your daddy know? He told me the other night over dinner that you were away at university."

"I am at university, and I am part of the Dyke Defenders," Sarah said, swallowing hard, deciding that she had to stand up for herself right there or never see her friends again. And the thought of not seeing Mary anymore because she had been banished from the Defenders was more than she could stand. Fuck the repercussions. She was in for the duration.

Mary looked over at her and smiled. Sarah had come a long way.

"Since you two are friends, why don't you invite us in for tea and the opponents can meet," Jane suggested.

"Are you serious?" Benton said, looking at Jane.

"It's about time, don't you think? This way when we meet again we'll be opponents and not enemies, per se."

"Yes, Benton. We should at least be cordial with one another. No need to be uncivilized. We'll leave the garbage can lids outside," Sarah said.

Jane nodded her approval.

The newscasters stood watching, not quite believing what was happening but gobbling it up. Jane knew they had made the evening news for sure. Benton ushered them in, and his assistant called room service.

"This is awesome," Bel whispered to Mary as they entered the posh hotel room.

"Different, that's for sure."

"But what are we going to talk about?" Bel asked.

"Jane will think of something, don't worry," Mary assured them.

Anne Beaumont took her Pernod and clicked on the television. Time for the news and some well-deserved relaxation. Her friend Holly Nelson sat next to her on the couch.

"You don't mind, do you? I just want to catch up."

"No, it's fine. I know you seldom turn off. I've known you too long."

They'd been college lovers, sorority sisters who

went too far. They both remembered those times with a certain fondness, albeit each woman recalled different things. Sometimes they were astounded at how differently they had perceived their relationship. Love renders you certifiably insane, Holly told her once. You can't see the forest because you don't see the tree until it hits you smack in the forehead. When you're on the ground with a severely bruised cranium, you begin to understand how you lost your way.

Anne was inclined to agree with her; however, she continued to make poor choices in lovers. Her career choices were touched with gold, while her love life stank like a barn in need of much attention. Still, she couldn't keep her clitoris in her pants, as Holly told her.

"Oh, my god, there she is," Anne said, pointing to the television.

"There who is?" Holly asked, looking blankly at the screen.

"Jane!"

"Who?" Holly asked.

"Jane, you know, the activist I told you about, young, dynamic, dangerous, and simply adorable."

"Jane? Let me guess, your latest infatuation."

"Yes," Anne said, becoming totally engrossed in the television.

"She doesn't have any hair."

"She shaves her head," Anne said, never taking her eyes off the television.

"Obviously. I didn't think you were attracted to those types of women."

"I'm not," Anne said.

"But . . ."

"Hair grows. Look, they got in to see Benton Peugh. How the hell did they manage that?" Anne pondered.

"I don't quite understand the attraction."

"Wait until you meet her. Do you remember Fiona Graves from school?"

"Attractive woman," Holly said.

"Very. Jane's her sister. I met her at a dinner party."

"She doesn't seem like dinner party material."

"It was at her sister's. I wonder if she liked the flowers I sent," Anne said.

"You sent her flowers?"

"Yes, it was an apology for making her angry. We went for coffee, I hit a nerve, and she told me to fuck off. So I sent flowers to try to smooth things over."

"Are you feeling okay?" Holly said, touching Anne's forehead. "You don't have a fever. You're not losing your mind, are you?"

"No, why?"

"No reason," Holly said, pouring them another Pernod.

"Must you do that now?" Louise asked, obviously perturbed.

"I'll only be a minute," Fiona said, flicking through the channels until she came to Channel 10 and set up the VCR to record. It was Jane's choice of newscasting, or rather she knew the staffers.

"We're in the middle of a dinner party."

"I'm aware of that. I'll be right there. Jane is protesting tonight, and I want to see if they air it. Is that all right?" Fiona said.

"What shall I tell everyone you're doing? Watching your psychotic sister getting arresting?"

"Do as you wish," Fiona said, turning around. The announcer introduced the story about the Defenders having tea with Peugh. Fiona saw Jane leading the pack in, and then as they were leaving she saw Adrienne snapping photos of the group with Benton Peugh. Strange bedfellows, stranger still that the Defenders ever got that close to Peugh. How did they do it? She stopped the frame with Adrienne in it. Her pulse quickened.

Carolyn came in.

"Is Jane on?"

"Yes. She had tea with Benton Peugh. I can only imagine what they talked about."

Carolyn stood next to her, catching one last glimpse of the Defenders as they marched in triumph for the Hyatt.

"I wish I had Jane's bravado," Carolyn said.

"Me too. It's not hereditary, as you've probably noticed."

"I'm not so sure about that. You have defied the hostess."

"True. Was it obvious?" Fiona asked.

"To put it mildly, yes," Carolyn said, sliding her glasses back up on her nose. Her soft brown eyes once again hid behind glass lenses.

"I'm sorry."

"Don't be. Louise should remember the old adage,

Blood is thicker than water. Never come between two sisters."

Fiona nodded.

"Look at us! We were absolutely stunning," Jane said, switching off the TV.

The Defenders were celebrating their feat with beer and pizza.

"I find it amazing that you got him to talk like that," Mary said.

"It only makes sense that as opponents we should understand each other's point of view without it being cut up and regurgitated by the press. He knows where we stand, and we know for certain what a hideous bigot, motherfucker, conservative bastard he is," Jane replied.

"I still can't believe he told us those things. Doesn't he think we're going to use them against him?" Adrienne said.

"He thinks we're harmless. And like any tragic hero, that is his crucial flaw. It's what will bring him tumbling down," Mary said, thinking suddenly in epic proportions. In some way, some day, they would bring him down. And then they would start in on his followers.

Six

"Not you again," Jane said, looking intently at the jar filled with strange liquid and something else, something unidentifiable.

"Did you like the flowers?" Anne asked, standing in the doorway dressed in a striking emerald green suit.

"Before or after I pitched them out the window?" Jane asked, setting the jar down, leaning on the table, and staring defiantly at Anne.

"Have you always been such a beast?" Anne asked.

"I morphed somewhere around my thirteenth year."

Anne tightened her jaw, pursed her lips, and sighed before speaking.

"I'm at a loss."

"So add something together and make yourself feel better."

"Jane, I find you extremely intriguing, and I'd just like the opportunity to get to know you. No strings, no hidden agendas, nothing. Just a simple friendship. I can't stop thinking about you, and if you'd give me a chance . . ."

Jane studied Anne and tried to measure her confession. Anne looked the picture of vulnerable, and Jane was a sucker for vulnerable. She could feel herself quivering inside. She hated wavering like this. Here was an attractive woman who was obviously interested in her, and the only thing separating them was political. Anne didn't know she was presenting Jane's nemesis: the quandary of getting personal with a woman who had an opposing political affiliation. Jane made herself jump, intuitively knowing that she'd have to do something to get Anne out of her system. The only way to do that was to kill desire, on both their parts. Jane smiled; it shouldn't be that hard.

"I admire honesty, above all else, I suppose. It's not always an easy thing to do. Perhaps we could try coffee again."

"Or dinner," Anne offered.

"Nothing fancier than a diner."

"All right, if you let me buy," Anne said.

"I drink a lot of wine at dinner," Jane teased.

"I'll bring a credit card."

"When?"

"Tomorrow night?" Anne said.

"All right."

"I'm looking forward to it."

"Do you own a T-shirt?" Jane asked.

"Yes," Anne said, looking puzzled.

"Will you wear it tomorrow?"

"If you'd like," Anne replied

"I'd like," Jane said, smiling.

Mary handed Jane a folder. She had been waiting all afternoon for her to arrive.

"Everything you always wanted to know but were afraid to ask."

"Meaning?"

"Anne Beaumont's profile. Industrious lady, I must say."

Jane set the folder down.

"Aren't you going to read it? I thought you'd be dying to."

"Later," Jane said, picking up the bottle of fluid again.

"Interesting stuff we carry around with us," Mary commented.

"What is it?"

"A malignant ovary."

"Where'd it come from?" Jane asked.

"Sarah is doing an art project where parts of the

body are to be abstracted. She chose female parts. She has a friend who is studying to be a pathologist at the Mayo Clinic. They borrowed it temporarily."

Jane studied the jar again, turning it to catch the light.

Mary watched her and got a queer feeling in her stomach.

"I can't believe it!" Fiona said, putting the phone back in its cradle. She swiveled in her chair and looked out the window. It was a gray, muggy day, and she suddenly longed for an endless blue sky. She felt tears well up. What is happening to us? she asked herself. We can't even have a civil conversation. It was the third time this week they had fought over stupid, trivial things.

There was a soft knock on the door frame. Fiona turned to see who it was. Adrienne looked puzzled.

"What's wrong?" she asked.

"Nothing," Fiona lied.

"You've been crying," Adrienne said, instantly wondering what Louise had done this time.

Fiona quickly wiped her eyes.

"Bad day?" Adrienne queried.

"Something like that."

"Want to talk about it?"

"I wouldn't know how to start," Fiona said, going to the window. Twilight was settling across the sky. Pink and gray laced the tumbled clouds. She used to love this time of day, when she was done with a run, going home to dinner, being happy to see Louise, and

looking forward to a steamy bath to ease aching
muscles and, sometimes, a steamy night, but now ...
now she dreaded going home. A house filled with
animosity, a house she couldn't wait to escape from
each day.

"Have you ever wondered how a love affair can
turn out so badly? How something once so beautiful
can get so ugly?" Fiona said, turning to look at
Adrienne.

Adrienne walked to her and gently took her in her
arms. Fiona closed her eyes and let their bodies meld.
It felt good to be held, to be touched by sympathetic
arms. She felt herself growing calm. Adrienne slowly
wiped the tears from her face, staring intently at her.

"Better?"

"Yes. I'm sorry. I didn't mean to burden you,"
Fiona said, turning away.

"You aren't. Don't ever think that. I want to help
if I can. It's not good to keep things bottled up inside.
Tears are the soul's only way of releasing the things
that hurt it."

"You mean I can't go to the doctor and say my
soul is hurting, can you give it a Band-Aid and a shot
of Novocain?" Fiona said.

"No. And you can't give it mouth to mouth.
Remember that," Adrienne said.

"Quick, her soul is bleeding. Get the tourniquet
before we lose her."

They both laughed.

"Are you hungry?" Adrienne asked.

Fiona didn't answer.

"Could you be made to be hungry? Take-out
Chinese food and a bottle of sake on the roof. Watch

119

the sunset and talk. You tell me your troubles, and I'll tell you mine," Adrienne asked, knowing she was crossing serious boundaries but unable to stop herself.

Fiona didn't relish the idea of going home to resume the argument that had ended with Louise getting frustrated and hanging up. Louise had never hung up on her before. Fiona felt shell-shocked.

Adrienne sensed she was persuadable.

"Come on. It'll do you good," Adrienne said, taking her hand and dragging her toward the door.

"Where are we going?"

"To get provisions. Lee Anne Chin's for the food, the corner liquor store for the beverage. Come on. You've never had the pleasure of shopping with me," Adrienne said, trying her best to be charming.

She was charming because she was shy. It made her all the more appealing. The argument would keep. Fiona would tell Louise she stayed late to cool off and get some work done. It would give Louise more time with her computer buddy.

"Adrienne, you're not a net surfer are you?"

"No. Why?"

"No reason, just curious."

Adrienne shrugged.

Holly answered the door to find Anne in a serious panic.

"Holly, do you have a T-shirt I could borrow?" Anne asked. After perusing her own closet, she discovered she had nothing of the sort and her dinner date was in less than an hour.

"A what?" Holly asked.

"A T-shirt."

"You don't have one?"

"It appears not, or I wouldn't be asking you," Anne said, slightly perturbed.

"Why do you need one? Are you going to work on your car, do a little gardening or, better yet, have a garage sale?" Holly chided.

"Do you have one or not?"

"What color?" Holly asked, taken aback by Anne's abruptness.

"I don't know, any color."

"You still haven't told me what for," Holly said, handing her a dark burgundy Guess T-shirt.

"A dinner date," Anne said, pulling on the shirt and tucking it into her slacks. She surveyed herself in the mirror.

"An informal one, I hope," Holly said.

"Don't you have one that's a little less pretentious?"

"Pretentious? How can a T-shirt be pretentious?" Holly asked.

"This is a designer T-shirt. I need a regular one."

"Who are you going to dinner with?"

"Jane," Anne replied.

"The one with no hair?"

"Yes," Anne said, rummaging in Holly's closet. She found a simple gray one. She pulled off one shirt and put the other one on while Holly tried without success not to stare at her breasts, which of course she was doing.

"You wouldn't happen to have a pair of jeans?" Anne asked.

Holly looked at her, puzzled, and handed her a pair of black Levi's.

"What are you doing, exactly?"

"Going to dinner with Jane," Anne said, putting the jeans on. They were a little big, but they'd work. She was going to have to go shopping for grunge wear if she was to stand a chance with Jane.

"You know what I mean," Holly said, her face laced with concern.

"Suffering through another one of my insane infatuations."

"She's not your type."

"I know, but maybe this time it'll be different."

"You're not serious," Holly said, sitting on the bed.

"I don't know. But I can't seem to get her out of my system. She's a graduate of Smith, you know."

"Meaning?" Holly asked, raising an eyebrow.

"She's not the street kid she pretends."

"Grooming potential?"

"I don't think so, and maybe that's a good thing," Anne said, sitting on the bed next to her.

"Have you been doing a little soul searching lately?" Holly said, tugging on the sleeve of Anne's shirt.

"Maybe I'm tired of playing the overeducated, uptight urban bitch."

"You've built a career on that image. What would be next?"

"I don't know yet, but when I do . . ."

"You'll let me know. I hope the ensemble proves acceptable."

"Thanks. It's me I'm worried about."

"Hmm . . ." Holly said, wishing she could shake some sense into her friend.

* * * * *

Fiona and Adrienne sat on a tattered blanket on the roof, eating Chinese food out of white paper containers and drinking sake out of Dixie cups. Louise would be horrified if she knew this was how she was spending her dinner hour, and this gave Fiona an exquisite sense of rebellion. Fiona wondered if she was suffering a midlife crisis, shirking her responsibilities and craving fun like a new designer drug.

"Have you tried this one?" Adrienne asked.

"Not yet."

Adrienne fed her a forkful of mysterious container number seven. They had decided to order with no knowledge of contents so that personal preference built on prior knowledge would be temporarily waylaid. It was Adrienne's idea.

"What about meat?" Fiona asked.

"What I don't know won't hurt me," Adrienne replied fearlessly.

"All right."

"Don't you think it's better this way? You try new things without fear because you set out on the journey for the sake of the experiment, not for attainment of the goal. We are much too goal oriented to reach the end rather than to rejoice in the means. The end should be viewed only as a jumping-off point for something new and not as a revered entity of ultimate achievement," Adrienne said.

Fiona raised an eyebrow. "It's no wonder Jane finds you so fascinating. I'm afraid that given the time and means, the two of you are quite capable of undermining most of Western civilization. You shall surely be imprisoned or martyred."

"A hundred years ago, that most certainly would have occurred. They would have put us in the loony bin. I'm not so sure we don't still belong there. And as for undermining civilization, I doubt we'll live up to your ideal. But anything is better than complacency, and I think we both need a place to put our energies to good use."

"Don't sell yourself short," Fiona said.

"What do you want to do with your life?"

"I think I'm past constructing ideas for a remarkable life."

"Because you're forty-something?" Adrienne said.

"Yes, I suppose," Fiona said, playing with her food.

"Why should that make a difference? You've got knowledge and experience behind you now. You're well seasoned."

"You make me sound like a dried-out turkey," Fiona chided.

"I didn't mean . . ." Adrienne stammered.

Fiona smiled. "I know you didn't. Here, try number eight."

The sun made a last shimmering effort before it dove into the far horizon. A flock of pigeons, frightened by something below, took flight. Fiona smiled at Adrienne, touching her cheek.

"Thank you for giving peace to a harried woman."

"Any time."

The Five and Diner was packed when Anne and Jane got there. Anne noticed that with Holly's grunge wear she fit right in. She breathed a sigh of relief.

"Nice shirt," Jane said, as they took their seats.

"Do I pass inspection?" Anne said, instantly regretting her words.

"It's not about inspection. I was curious to see if you owned one," Jane said, picking up a menu. "Although I wouldn't be surprised if you had to borrow it."

Anne blushed.

Jane smiled. "I figured as much. What sort of a woman has to borrow a T-shirt?"

"I never thought I needed one until now."

"Perhaps that'll change," Jane said, looking up at the extremely tall waitress. "How many bottles of wine are we ordering?"

"Three bottles of merlot."

"Will it go with dinner?" Jane inquired.

"It doesn't matter."

"This should be interesting," Jane said, putting the menu down. "I'll have a hamburger with french fries."

"The same," Anne told the waitress.

"If I didn't know better, I'd think you were trying to please me."

"I'm not," Anne lied.

"Good."

"I should go," Fiona said, looking at her watch. She got up from the creaky lawn chair and took a last look at the glittering skyline.

"I'll walk you out," Adrienne said, wishing the night wasn't over.

They stood by Fiona's car.

"I had fun tonight," Fiona said.

"Me too," Adrienne said

"We'll have to do it again," Fiona said, hoping she didn't sound like she was making empty promises.

"People will talk."

"And what will they say?" Fiona asked, not really wanting to know.

"Probably not good things," Adrienne said, staring at her.

"I don't care. Can I have a hug?" Fiona said.

Jane and Anne came around the corner. Jane grabbed Anne's arm.

"What?"

"Shh," Jane said, making her stand back. "Look," she said, pointing to the parking lot. In the dim flood of the streetlight they saw Adrienne and Fiona wrapped in an embrace.

"Isn't that Fiona?"

"Hmm . . ."

"Who is the other woman?"

"It's Adrienne."

"Your cute little friend that I met at Louise's dinner party?"

"Yes. So you think she's cute, huh?" Jane teased.

"Not as cute as you."

"You've had too much to drink," Jane said flatly.

"You've had more. So are they committing adultery?"

"That depends on what sort of system you subscribe to. Come on, let's leave them alone."

"You don't want to stop it?" Anne asked.

"It's not my place to stop it. Fiona's a big girl, and Louise is far from my favorite person. If Sis wants to play around . . ."

"Do you play around?" Anne said. She half stumbled up the stairs.

"I'm calling you a cab."

Jane turned on the desk lamp and went to get a Coke. Her wine hangover was nipping viciously at her heels. She was dreading her next move, but it had to be done.

"You didn't answer my question," Anne said, as she sat down on the desktop, sending the jar that was sitting there flying to the floor. "What was that?"

"A specimen," Jane said, gently kicking the squishy red thing with the toe of her sneaker.

"I'm sorry," Anne said.

"It's all right. I'm sure we can get more. I have a question for you."

"Yes?"

"How is it that you've gone from a staff writer for *Teen* magazine to a lesbian feminist bent on turning patriarchy inside out with a swish of your pretty hand?"

"How did you know about that?" Anne said, instantly mortified.

"It's one of the marvels of modern technology and diligent assistants," Jane said snidely.

"Can you get me a towel so I can clean this up?" Anne said.

"It'll keep. Answer the question."

"People aren't born feminists. It's a process of evolution. At that point in my life I wanted a career in journalism, and I didn't care how I got it," Anne replied, feeling her stomach churn in a less-than-desirable fashion.

"Even at the price of fucking with impressionable young minds and contributing to the further subjugation of womankind?" Jane said, going in for the kill.

"Jane, please," Anne begged.

"The truth is ugly."

"Doesn't it make any difference that I spent the rest of my career trying to remedy the situation?"

"I suppose. I couldn't believe it, though. I've stood in front of those magazine racks and studied how patriarchy begins the training, and to find out that you were a part of it . . ."

"It's not like you thought I was wonderful to begin with," Anne said.

"I was suspicious of your methods because you're part of the movement that frowns on us, but it doesn't mean I didn't respect you."

"And you don't now?" Anne asked, knowing it was a stupid question.

"Now, I wonder about your motives," Jane said, growing angry.

"I want to help make things better," Anne pleaded.

"For all women or just for yourself?" Jane asked.

"Jane, that's not fair. Why won't you give me a chance?"

"Why do you want one?" Jane asked, glaring at her.

"Why do you always answer a question with a question?"

"I'm calling you a cab," Jane said, picking up the phone and giving the dispatcher the address.

Anne felt like a truant schoolgirl. This was so unlike her, but she couldn't stop the rushing cascade of feelings she had toward Jane, and if she didn't do something fast she was going to lose all chance of seeing her again.

"Why do we fight all the time?"

"Because opposites attract," Jane said, hating herself for saying it.

"Are you attracted?" Anne asked hopefully.

Jane looked at her. "No, I'm not."

The cab honked outside, and Jane walked her out.

"Jane . . ." Anne began.

"Get in," Jane said, opening the door.

Anne bit her lip, nodded, and got in the cab.

Jane hit the door with her fist as she went indoors. This was going to be harder than she thought.

Claudette, sleeping quietly with Eddy the cat nestled about her feet, looked like an angel. Jane lit a cigarette and studied the outline of her lover's body, the gentle curve of her hip, the rising swell of her breast, the smoothness of her neck, the firm line of her jaw. How long had she been doing this, staying out late to come in and discover Claudette's body anew? And why did it take other women to remind her of her desire for Claudette? What sort of love affair was it that required a placebo first and then reality?

Her mind kept moving back through the night. What did Anne want with her? Why had she come into her life? All Jane wanted was simplicity, domestic tranquillity, and sisterhood. She knew Anne Beaumont was not going to give her those things. She snuggled up to Claudette, kissing her neck, running her hand down her stomach. Claudette rolled over and kissed her.

"How was dinner?" she asked, sleepily.

"I missed you tonight," Jane said, feeling urgency creep into her voice.

"Show me," Claudette said, gruffly reaching for Jane.

Fiona was sitting on the end of Mary's long worktable littered with stacks of papers, pop cans, and the ever-present hum of Mary's mega computer, which Fiona swore made the table vibrate with its energy. It made Fiona nervous just looking at the setup. She half expected the computer to take off one day like a small-engine plane using the table as a runway. She preferred her good old three-eighty-six with its simple system of operation.

"You sent this to one of those rag publications?" Fiona asked as Mary showed her the steps to scanning and recreating Benton's photograph.

"We certainly did," Mary said, beaming with subversive pride.

"You girls are dangerous. It's grounds for libel you know," Fiona said, taking a sip of coffee.

"They have to catch us first."

"More coffee?" Fiona asked, holding the pot.

"Sure. You're up and about awfully early. And I bet you've been running already," Mary said.

"I was having trouble sleeping," Fiona said, thinking she'd got home late and then lay awake for hours listening to Louise breathe, wondering just what the hell she was doing with her life. And this thing with Adrienne wasn't going to make it any easier. Up to now she could call it a friendship, but after they held each other tightly, bodies touching too close for too long, could she still call it that? It was better to get up and go running. She couldn't bring herself to face Louise, so she hightailed it after a quick shower.

Adrienne, Claudette, and Jane came in carrying a bag of bagels, a tub of cream cheese, and a jug of orange juice.

"Breakfast of champions," Jane said.

"You're in a good mood," Fiona commented. "Dinner with Anne Beaumont never puts me in anything close to a good mood."

"Oh, that! That was a perfect disaster. It was dessert that altered my mood," Jane said, grabbing Claudette and kissing her neck.

Adrienne smiled at Fiona, knowing they were both going to feel awkward after last night. Adrienne was determined to let Fiona make the moves, if there were any to be made. It would save them both a lot of grief. Adrienne also had sat up late into the night thinking, only to discover it was better not to. She wished she could talk to Jane. Jane would know what to do. But she couldn't. Somewhere deep down she knew that this was one of the few things Jane wouldn't approve of.

They began the game of stuffing their mouths with bagels to see who could fit the most bagel in.

"Someone is going to choke," Fiona warned. Jane ripped off a piece of her bagel and stuffed it in Fiona's mouth.

"That's not fair," Fiona started to say.

"Life's not fair. Now get stuffing," Jane said.

Jane painted a cream cheese mustache on her face and then one on Claudette's. Adrienne won the contest with a bagel and a half. Jane was duly impressed. Fiona had barely finished getting her bagel swallowed when Louise came in. Their jocularity evaporated immediately, as if someone's mother had come home unexpectedly and the party was over.

"Would you like a bagel?" Claudette offered.

"No thank you. I've already eaten. I came to see if my wife would like to have lunch since I missed having breakfast with her," Louise said, trying to avoid an icy tone but knowing it came out that way.

"Have a cup of coffee at least," Claudette said, handing her one.

Louise stepped forward and took it. Jane looked down at Louise's expensive boots standing in goop and the toe of her boot quickly soaking up the excess fluid from the still moist ovary as it nestled against it. Louise followed Jane's gaze.

"What on earth!" she said, taking a quick step backward.

"Whoops, I forgot to clean that up last night," Jane said, grabbing a paper towel.

"What is it? Is it going to come off my shoes?" Louise said, color rising to her face.

Fiona watched the familiar series of moves from social etiquette to complete rage as they tumbled through Louise's demeanor.

"It's an ovary," Jane said.

"It's a what?" Louise screeched.

"An ovary," Jane replied calmly.

The canoe and rider went sailing over the edge of

the waterfall. Louise was pissed. Adrienne looked over at Fiona who, to her surprise, did not look alarmed. Rather, she was glancing at her watch as if she was calculating how much longer Louise was going to remain in the room.

"I am standing on an ovary. Only in this den of iniquity would a person be subjected to such hideousness. What is an ovary doing here? I don't want to know. Fiona, if you choose to consort with such degenerates, that is your business. But count me out, and forget lunch!" Louise said, storming from the room and leaving a set of dark footprints in her wake.

"I'll take you to lunch, darling," Jane said, before they all burst out laughing, Fiona included.

"I think we should leave the footprints right where they are," Jane said, getting a can of spray shellac from the cupboard. "A testimony to will, fire, and anger," she said, spraying the marks evenly.

Sarah came in after her early class. Mary gave her a bagel, and she sat happily munching it while they filled her in on the morning's events.

"You know, this gives me an idea," Sarah said. She was staring at the organ still lying unceremoniously on the floor.

"Oh no. I can hardly wait," Jane said, going for the broom and the dustpan.

"What if I could get a bunch of ovaries and we let them all loose on the steps of the capitol just before Benton Peugh is scheduled to leave? What more poignant message could we give than having him walk through the organs of women as he goes about organizing legislation designed to enslave our bodies. We'll give him the part he wants most," Sarah said.

133

The room stood quiet.

"You're a genius," Jane said, incredulity written across her face. "A fucking genius!"

"Maybe she's tapped into the Mother herself, acting as some kind of agent of the Goddess," Claudette said.

Mary looked at Sarah with utter pride. "Can you get more?"

"I think so. I'll need Bel's van."

"I'm sure we can persuade Bel to drive the getaway car," Adrienne said.

"Sis, will you come to this rally? This is going to be a big one, the biggest one, and I really want you to be there."

Fiona looked at Adrienne and Jane, knowing she couldn't refuse. "Yes. I may even open a jar or two myself, despite my usually squeamish nature."

"Jane, wait! Let me get my camera so we document the inception of the idea. Sarah, go stand by Jane with the ovary. The masterminds at work," Adrienne said, grabbing her now ever-present camera.

"So how did it go?" Holly asked, as she poured a red vinaigrette over her salad. She was sitting at the kitchen bar in Anne's high-rise apartment.

"It was awful," Anne said, pouring herself another glass of wine.

"The T-shirt wasn't successful?"

"No, it was me. It didn't start out badly but it ended badly. Dinner was nice. We talked, not about politics, rather about love."

"You talked about love?" Holly said, trying to image Anne's bald dinner companion having a sensitive moment.

"Love affairs, our first ones. You know, the stupid kinds you have in college when everyone is awkward and does goony things."

"Thanks a lot!"

"Holly, I didn't mean us. We were good, very good. Well, you were good. I was the stupid one," Anne said, coming up behind Holly and giving her a hug.

"Sometimes I wish we had met later, so we could have gotten old together," Holly said, her brisk blue eyes diving into Anne's soft gray ones.

"We will get old together," Anne assured her.

"You know what I mean," Holly said, turning away.

"I do. I'm sorry I was such a shit."

"You weren't."

"I was," Anne admitted, running quickly through her catalog of sins.

"What are you going to do about your new friend?" Holly said, changing the subject because she suddenly felt awkward for confessing what she liked to keep properly buried. She admitted to occasionally putting a bouquet of flowers on the grave of their dead love affair, but she seldom spoke of it.

"There isn't anything to do. I botched it."

"How exactly did you botch it?" Holly asked.

"She found out about my days at *Teen*."

Holly made a queer face. "Not good."

"No."

"I thought that was a well-kept secret."

"It's supposed to be," Anne said, thankful she had had the foresight even then to use a pen name.

"And you apologized profusely?" Holly said, picking at her salad, thinking she wasn't hungry anymore.

"On the verge of prostration."

"I don't know what to tell you. Send flowers," Holly said.

"She threw the last bunch out of a second-story window."

"Are you sure you want to associate with such an individual?"

Anne looked at her friend and immediately understood her attraction to Jane. It was her passionate response to living. Knowing people wasn't about *associating*: It was about connection, infatuation, lust, and love, not tidy pigeonholes of emotions that could be conveniently closed off if they proved unsuitable.

"Holly, I'm hooked," Anne confessed.

"Perhaps you should discuss this with your therapist."

"I have an appointment this afternoon."

"Good," Holly said, handing her the bread.

Jane had walked around the block four times. Thoughts of Anne were driving her crazy. She silently cursed the universe for being so perverse as to not honor her wish to forget. She couldn't get the woman out of her head. It was like Anne had come for dinner and never left. It seemed she'd taken up residence in the guest quarters of Jane's mind without an invitation. Jane kept playing back the night before, how Anne held her glass, her long, cool fingers when they accidentally touched reaching for the ketchup, and those gray eyes. She was a beautiful woman.

There was no doubting that. Did Jane pick fights with Anne because she was attracted to her and was playing the antagonist by keeping her at arm's length? She had handled many a difficult woman before, but never one like this. She felt the bad vibes her intuition sent out as fair warning, but they didn't prevent her from putting a quarter in the pay phone and dialing the number Anne had written on the matchbook cover. All capitals, and the numbers perfectly square.

"Hi."

"Jane?"

"None other. Listen, I'm sorry about last night. I was rude, extremely rude."

Anne pressed the phone to her ear tighter and closed her eyes.

"Jane?"

"Hmm . . ."

"Can we try again?"

"Perhaps another attempt might prove more successful. If you'd like, I want you to come to the rally we have planned for Benton Peugh's performance before the legislature," Jane said, feeling her face flush and hating it.

"When?"

"Three weeks from now on Tuesday night."

Anne flipped through her Day-Timer looking frantically for the date. She didn't care what she had planned, she'd cancel it.

"I'd love to."

"Good, we'll see you then."

"Jane?"

"Yes?"

"Could I perhaps see you again before then?"

"If you'd like," Jane said, swallowing hard.

"We could try another meal, perhaps lunch this time. It might work out better. Say Friday?"

"Sure," Jane said, pressing her head against the glass of the phone booth.

"Is the Loring Café okay?" Anne queried.

"Yeah, it's great. But you have to let me buy this time."

"Did I tell you I drink a lot of wine with lunch?"

"I'll bring a lot of money," Jane said.

"I can't wait," Anne said.

"I promise to behave myself, or at least make a gallant effort."

"Don't. I like you just the way you are."

"You say that now . . ."

Anne sat down with the phone in her lap, feeling like a starstruck schoolgirl. Then she thought of the "we" that Jane had spoken of. It wasn't the first time she'd dated a married woman but it was the first time she cared. This was more than flirtation, infidelity, and consummation.

She went to Target and bought twenty-five T-shirts and seven pairs of jeans. She came home and threw them in the washer, trying to calculate how many times she could get them washed before she saw Jane again. Anne didn't question her motives. She put herself on autopilot and ignored her therapist's advice to stop her silly infatuation that would end badly if she pursued it. For once she felt reckless. And she kind of liked it.

Seven

Fiona ran up around the Walker Art Museum; hills were good leg builders, and the physiological details kept her mind from roaming. This was her eighth consecutive time up the hill. She was shooting for twenty. The security guard in his little booth had begun to take notice of her apparently pathological behavior.

She could hardly look at Louise for fear her face would give her secret away. The night before when

Louise tried to make amends for the fight and the episode at the office, Fiona just nodded, took her glass of wine and the latest book she was supposed to be reviewing, and went outside on the veranda. July had finally arrived, and the twilight hour was sprinkled with warmth and the promise of humidity. Louise followed. She wrapped her arms around Fiona and kissed her ear. Fiona had pulled away.

"Can't we let it go?" Louise asked.

"I already have."

"Why are you so cold then?"

"I just need some space, that's all. I'm fine really."

Louise stood up, puzzled. "All right. I'll make dinner then."

"Okay."

They looked at each other. Fiona tried to smile, but she read hurt in Louise's eyes. Any other time she would have gotten up, given her a hug, and whispered reassurances, but this time she found herself numb, frozen in inertia. What was happening to them?

When she got home her legs were burning and her body sweating. She grabbed a bottle of water from the fridge. Louise had a meeting. The house was empty. She picked up Einstein, the silver tabby, and wandered toward the den. The book review was still unwritten. Perhaps now was a good time to get started, she thought. No time like the present, her mother's words popped into her head. I should call her, she mused. You should write the review, her conscience corrected her.

Fiona put the cat down on the desk and switched on the computer. Einstein rubbed against the monitor while it clicked and hummed. She logged on and checked her e-mail. She'd wanted to write her editor a quick note to let her know the review was on its way. In the middle of her note, a message popped up from the buddy list.

Hi, darling are you there? the buddy typed in.

Fiona was confused. She didn't usually work at home. The computer at home was Louise's domain. For half a second she thought it might be Louise, and then she remembered the computer buddy. Louise was such a whiz with the computer. Fiona used to joke with her about loving the analytical stuff more than the emotional side of life. Computers could be controlled and manipulated unlike people.

I was hoping you'd be there, the stranger typed in.

I just got home. How are you? Fiona replied, wondering if she could pull this off. She'd have to put on her best Louise act. She knew it well, the diction, the cadence, the language of her wife. Sometimes she wondered if she didn't know Louise better than herself. Was this knowing too much part of the problem? She had almost lost herself again when more words crossed the screen asking her about her weekend. Fiona aka Louise recounted the events beautifully. She reciprocated as she knew Louise politely would. The mystery companion did likewise. It all seemed innocent enough until the normal social courtesies turned to a more romantic mood, a strange computer language of erotic statements.

Shall we go to a private chat room?

Okay, Fiona typed in. She followed the mystery woman's lead into the chat room.

I was having a bath and thinking of you.

What were you thinking? Fiona asked, knowing it could be a harmless albeit leading question.

I was thinking about your long, cool fingers inside me.

Fiona had just taken a drink of water. She spat all over the computer. "Shit!" she said, running to the kitchen for a towel.

Are you still there?

I spilled water on the computer.

I'm sorry. I love it when you get nervous. You're always so cute when you do that.

Aren't you going to tell me more?

I love it when you say that. Of course, you want more, don't you? Tell me you do.

I do. I want more.

The mystery woman went on to catalog a variety of activities that alarmed Fiona. She felt like what Louise must feel when she was around Jane and the other Defenders. Fiona tried to live up to her part. She started to get lost in what kind of things Louise would come up with in this bizarre drama. The woman seemed used to this.

Just tell me what you were thinking, then what you did. I know you're shy. I'll help you along just like I always do, right?

Right. Fiona frantically tried to come up with her best masturbating fantasies. Suddenly, and quite surprisingly, she thought of Adrienne and what she would do with her. She began to type in her fantasy. The front door clicked and she heard Louise.

Oh, shit!

She's home.

Yes.

Well, darling, coitus interruptus. But I shall certainly be looking forward to tomorrow. Bye, my love.

Fiona rapidly closed files and tried to extricate herself from the room.

"What are you up to?" Louise asked, as Fiona bumped into her in the hall.

"I was just trying to do something with that book review," Fiona stammered.

"You're all flushed. Do you feel all right?" Louise asked, putting her hand to Fiona's forehead.

"Hmm . . . I was running hills."

"How was your day?" Louise asked, looking past her and into the den.

"It was fine. Did you go shopping?"

"Yes, just some stuff for dinner."

"Let me help you."

"There's only one bag left."

"I'll get it."

Louise didn't argue. Fiona left. Louise went to the computer and touched the back of the monitor. It was warm. She felt her heart quicken. Fiona couldn't have . . . Louise thought, This is not good.

She found Fiona in the kitchen putting groceries away.

"I wanted to make something nice for dinner."

"You always make nice dinners," Fiona said, her head in the fridge.

"Something special to make up for things," Louise said.

"I'm sorry about behaving badly lately," Fiona said,

trying to get the knot out of her throat. Part of her felt sickened at what she had just experienced, but the other half was fearful at the thought of losing Louise.

"Me too. Can we let it go?" Louise asked, pulling Fiona to her.

"Please," Fiona said, kissing her. They kissed again, deeper this time, as if their bodies were remembering a time when being physical could be a lover's most precious balm. Louise pushed Fiona against the fridge, pressing her body close, sliding her thigh between Fiona's legs. She kissed her neck and ran her hands along the waistline of Fiona's running shorts. Fiona's breath quickened with each move Louise made.

"This is kind of different," Fiona said, thinking that Louise didn't often make first moves. She used to, but somehow as they had gotten older those ardent days of youth seemed long past. It had been Louise, after all, who had first seduced Fiona, much like what was happening right now.

"I want you," Louise said, looking straight into Fiona's eyes.

"I need a shower," Fiona said, starting to pull away, feeling uncomfortable with this sudden change in sexual tactics.

"No, you need me," Louise said, lifting up Fiona's T-shirt and kissing her stomach. Louise maneuvered her over to the couch, removing Fiona's clothes as she went.

"Don't you want to go upstairs?"

"No, I want to stay right here," Louise said, spreading Fiona's legs and lowering herself between them.

Fiona's protests were lost in a full mouth and soft

cries. Louise scrambled to get her clothes off; neither was able to get enough of the other quickly enough, like old times, when making love was the focus of every day. Louise was making her come, and Fiona was crying. Then Louise quivered and fell. With hands still inside each other, they lay together.

"Why are you crying?" Louise asked, frightened that Fiona was going to tell her that she'd found out about Kimberly.

"I've missed you," Fiona said, pulling her tight.

"I'm sorry," Louise said, meaning it, thinking she shouldn't haven't started the whole insane thing with a stranger when all she really wanted was to fall madly in love with her wife again.

Later that night Fiona lay awake, thinking about making love. Did Louise think of her computer buddy when she touched her? Hadn't the image of Adrienne crossed her mind when she lay with her face nestled between Louise's legs? Who were they really making love to? Were they just instruments of lust to each other now? Fiona felt tears run down the side of her face. Should she ask Louise about her cybersex afternoons or should she let it go? Questions spun in her head. She lay awake until the first light of dawn. She crept from bed and put her running clothes on.

The morning was crisp and the light was soft and pink as she headed across the park. At this hour the city was quiet, the breeze rustled the leaves, and the slow ventilators on the buildings droned methodically. Her shoes made the rhythmic sound she loved. The even thud, thud of her feet and her breath, two in and two out. It was all neat, controlled, and measurable. She ran mile after mile until it seemed she was running on automatic. Her mind lulled into a stupor of breath and muscle, her body running to a place where thought was no longer possible.

When she got back, she kissed Louise sweetly as if nothing was wrong and carried on a pleasant breakfast conversation. She left for work, wondering on the way out the door if she'd lost her mind.

She felt empty. In the past they would have had a good row about this little transgression, got it off their chests, cried, made incredible love, and moved on, content in the knowledge that it was over. It wasn't as though through the years they hadn't had women come between them, brief flirtations, but nothing like this. Were they finally coming to an end? She couldn't imagine life without Louise, but how could they possibly continue this way?

The book review sat half attempted while Fiona lay sleeping with her head on the desk. Jane studied her sister's face from across the room. She was a beautiful woman, but then their father was a handsome man and their mother an attractive woman. It was odd coming from the same deep, dark womb, both made from the same parts, nurtured on the same blood, and yet unique. They were different, but having shared most of their lives, they had achieved a sameness by virtue of experience. Jane drank her coffee and wondered what Fiona was up to.

She kept thinking back to the night she had seen Fiona and Adrienne in the parking lot. Was Fiona fucking Adrienne? Somehow, Jane couldn't quite picture it, but anything was possible in this wicked world. She found it hard to face that image. Fiona and Louise had always inspired her, much as she avoided mentioning it. They had a long love, something Jane respected. It couldn't fall apart just like that. You can't walk away from fourteen years for a girl in the parking lot, Jane thought. What about love and memories?

She couldn't picture anything lasting between Fiona and Adrienne, and she didn't understand the attraction. But who was she to wonder when she didn't understand her own attraction to Anne. Now there's a coupling, Jane thought, smirking.

Fiona woke up, blinking from the afternoon light filling her office.

"What time is it?"

"Eleven-thirty," Jane answered, thinking she needed to leave soon.

"I must have dozed off."

"No shit. Most people sleep at night. What have you been doing with yours?"

"Lying awake," Fiona said, rubbing her eyes.

"A small bout of insomnia?"

"Something like that."

"What's going on?" Jane asked.

"I wish I knew," Fiona said, letting out a long sigh.

"If you ever need to talk . . ." Jane queried, arching an eyebrow.

"Oh, Jane, it's all such a mess I wouldn't even know where to begin."

"Try me."

In her mind Fiona rattled off a list of woes: I'm

infatuated with your best friend, which is utterly ridiculous for a woman my age. My wife is having cybersex afternoons with a perfect stranger while I'm pretending to be faithful and devoted when I feel quite the contrary. And on top of that I am unable to complete something as simple as a book review because I can't concentrate long enough to get it done. So instead she came up with, "My Achilles tendon is killing me from running."

"You used to tell me things."

"I can't right now," Fiona said.

"Maybe the Achilles tendon is really an Achilles heel. Watch out for arrows and Greeks bearing gifts, big sister."

"I will."

"Okay, I'm off," Jane said, giving her sister a long look.

"Where to?"

"Lunch with Anne Beaumont," Jane said, avoiding her sister's gaze.

"I thought you didn't like her."

"So did I."

"If you ever need to talk ..."

"I think when the smoke clears we'll have some really good stories to tell each other," Jane said.

"Hmm ..."

Jane sat waiting for Anne at the Loring Café. She couldn't remember the first time she'd been early for a date. She was usually the one who came straggling in without so much as a meager apology. She figured it was part of her Zen timekeeping philosophy: You got there when you were supposed to get there. So what did being early mean? she asked herself.

Anne was surprised to find her there.

"Hi."

"Is this table okay?" Jane asked.

"It's wonderful," Anne said, taking a seat.

"I took the liberty of choosing the wine," Jane said, pouring them both a glass.

"Thank you," Anne said.

They ordered lunch and tried to get through some awkward conversation until Anne couldn't stand it anymore and blurted out the question that was forefront in her mind.

"How long have you and Claudette been together?"

Jane poured them more wine.

"Why do you ask?" Jane said, knowing where this question was going.

"Have you ever been to therapy?"

"No. Why? Do I act like I have?" Jane asked.

"Perhaps."

"What does that mean?"

"Have your ever heard of hyperanalytical lesbianism?" Anne inquired.

"No, but I get the feeling I'm going to."

"Answering a question with a question is a case in point," Anne replied.

"We've been together for four years," Jane said.

"Are you happy?" Anne asked, not certain what kind of a response she wanted.

"I don't like that term. It's hard to define."

"Content?" Anne asked.

"Same difference."

"You're impossible."

"Thank you," Jane said, smiling coyly.

* * * * *

It was almost dark, and they were sitting on top of one of the picnic tables in the park. They had watched the people having clandestine affairs meet in the early afternoon. After five o'clock they watched the runners do laps through the park, followed by people diligently walking their dogs. They decided that most owners and animals resembled one another, morphed in either direction. Then they watched the businesspeople drag themselves to the parking lots to go home and begin the second part of their daily charade.

"Do you realize we've spent most of the afternoon together and haven't had one argument?" Anne said.

"The day is not over yet," Jane teased.

"Why did we get off to such a rocky start?"

"Because you're everything I don't like in a lesbian," Jane said flatly.

"Are you always this brutally honest, or do you reserve this banter for me alone?"

"You're special to me."

"What does that mean?" Anne asked, her stomach doing an instant backflip.

"I'm intrigued. At first I was simply disgusted. Now I want to know more. It's time for a couple of confessions. You tell me a few choice and embarrassing episodes in your life, and I'll do the same."

"Why do we want to do this?" Anne inquired.

"You're the one in therapy. You should know."

"Well, I don't. Enlighten me," Anne replied.

"You can tell a lot about a person by what she confesses."

"Like what?"

Jane rolled her eyes. "Think about it. We

remember things that mark us in some way. Those incidents go into making up who we are, and that's what makes them important confessions. What you tell is who you are."

"I'm feeling a lot of pressure with this," Anne said, swallowing hard.

"Hanging out with me will always be a challenge. Are you ready to take the first dare?" Jane said, staring at her intently, the flame of challenge burning in her eyes.

"All right," Anne said, silently praying she would choose the right confession.

Claudette and Adrienne finished unloading the jars of feminine body parts from the back of Bel's van. The jars lined one entire wall and gave the office an eerie aquariumlike glow. Sarah had to go to class, and Bel had been picked up by a very attractive woman named Mitsy in a white Mustang convertible.

"Where the hell is Jane?" Claudette asked.

"It is odd. It's not like her to forget something as important as this," Adrienne said, handing her a beer.

Claudette lit a cigarette and stood looking at the wall of ovaries. Adrienne got her camera.

Claudette turned, blowing her smoke out slowly. "What are you doing?"

"Stay there," Adrienne said, focusing the camera.

"Photodocumenting?"

"Yep."

"Adrienne, are you in love with Fiona?"

Adrienne's mouth dropped open before she could stop herself. "Does it look like I am?"

"Yes."

"You shouldn't be," Claudette replied matter-of-factly, as if she were advising Adrienne on some banal activity she should really give up.

"I know. I can't *help* it."

"Fiona will never leave Louise."

"I know."

"Be careful with your heart," Claudette said, putting her arm around Adrienne's shoulders and nestling her head in the crook of Adrienne's neck. They both felt a wave of warmth and security that temporarily lulled the barrage of longing that was knocking at both their hearts: one for what she knew she was losing and the other for what she knew she couldn't have. They stood that way longer than they should have.

Claudette took Adrienne by the shoulders and shook her gently, trying to keep the pain she was feeling from clouding the landscape of her face.

"This is not going to be fun," she said.

Adrienne nodded, knowing she was speaking as much of herself as she was of Adrienne's predicament.

Except for the small green desk light by Mary's computer it was dark in the office when Jane got back. She looked at the wall and remembered the appointment she'd forgotten. She felt ashamed.

"Love is tyranny of the worst sort," Jane said out loud.

"Why do you say that?" a voice asked in darkness.

Jane turned. "What are you doing here?" she asked Fiona.

"Thinking," Fiona said.

"Shouldn't you be home?"

"Yes."

"Then why aren't you?" Jane asked, trying to make out her sister's features in the half-light of the room.

"Because I've been running at the club."

"The track on the roof?" Jane asked.

"Yes."

"I can't believe you still have a membership at that heinous bourgeois establishment."

"It's the only safe place a woman can run at night."

"For the love of running . . ."

"Have to love something," Fiona said flatly.

Jane grabbed two beers from the fridge and sat down on the couch next to Fiona. She looked down at Fiona's feet. Her socks were soaked in blood.

"What have you done to yourself?"

"Nothing," Fiona said, feeling utterly numb, which had been her intent. She couldn't remember how many times she'd run around the track. She'd quit when the security guard came to tell her they were closing.

"Your feet . . ." Jane said, kneeling down and gently pulling off her sister's socks. Fiona's feet were blistered and bleeding.

"I don't know what's wrong, but you've got to stop this shit," Jane said, getting some hydrogen peroxide and Band-Aids from the cupboard. Fiona drank her beer and stared off into space while Jane fixed her feet.

"Why are you doing this?" Jane said, unable to keep anger from creeping into her voice.

"I'm losing it, Jane. I feel like I don't know anything about myself anymore. I do things. I think things I would never think myself capable of."

"Maybe you've been invaded by an alien," Jane muttered, trying to unstick the Band-Aid from her own fingers to put it on Fiona. First aid was not her forte.

Fiona burst out laughing. "That's the best answer I've heard yet."

"No really, Fiona, remember when you were in grad school and you had that rough spot?"

"Yes."

"What did you do then?"

"I went to see Dad, and he talked me through it. He made me see that everything you experience is capable of teaching you something and that if you can learn to look at it that way you'll never go crazy because you grow, and growth and challenge are what makes life worth living."

"Exactly."

"I don't see how it fits here."

"Maybe you're going through some growing pains with Louise right now, and either you can let it drive you crazy or you can learn from it."

"Jane, what if I'm falling in love with someone else?"

"Then take it where it leads you, but don't let it destroy you."

"But it'll destroy my relationship with Louise."

"Not necessarily."

Fiona looked at her puzzled.

"Things happen for a variety of reasons. Most of which are not immediately revealed. If you're in love, follow it and fuck the consequences."

"If it was meant to happen it will?"

"Yes. If you're capable of falling in love you're just as capable of falling out. You're human, Fiona. It happens."

Eight

Fiona and Anne were huddled in the back of Bel's van along with the rest of the Dyke Defenders.

"This is definitely odd," Fiona said, looking over at Anne.

"I offered to drive," Anne replied, thinking it would have been much more comfortable in her tasteful green Range Rover.

"Let me guess who decided this was the more proper way to be involved," Fiona said.

Anne nodded. She smiled in Jane's direction. Both

156

Fiona and Claudette watched, puzzled. If love can be written across a face, it was. Claudette felt her stomach tighten. This was different from the others. Fiona caught Claudette's shoulder and squeezed it gently.

"It all comes out in the wash, right?" Fiona said.

"Except shit and blood," Claudette said, turning to stare out the window.

"Perhaps," Fiona said, thinking that she was doing the same thing to Louise that Jane was doing to Claudette; being dishonest, pretending things were other than what they were. Why couldn't they talk anymore? It was like they were going through empty motions, pretending to be together when they no longer were. She never thought she would feel so alone and yet go home every night to her lover. But she did. It was eating at her, and she fervently prayed for someone to snatch the gnawing little creature from her heart.

Jane took a corner fast, and the jars clanked in the back.

"Jane, we won't make much of a scene if the ovaries are all over the van instead of the steps of the capital," Mary said as she tried to right the fallen bottles.

"Sorry," Jane yelled into the back of the van. She winked at Anne. Claudette saw and pressed her head hard against the windowpane.

Louise sat at the computer with a glass of wine. She didn't normally drink alone. But nothing seemed normal anymore. She clicked on the monitor and waited. It was the appointed hour and Kimberly didn't disappoint her.

"Hello, darling. How are you? I must say you were absolutely stunning yesterday. You are definitely developing. But we're not finished, are we?" Kimberly typed in.

Louise snapped off the monitor, closed her eyes, and felt a wave of nausea sweep across her. Fiona knew. She picked up the waste can and threw up. She walked away, forgetting to turn off the modem.

Bel locked up the van with its precious cargo. She set the boom box on top of the van, and the predemonstration party and picnic began.

"Is this how you usually conduct a demonstration?" Anne asked as she helped Jane lay the checkered oilcloth across the picnic tables.

"Yes, complete with rutabaga tacos," Jane said as Mary unloaded the ice chest.

"Did you say what I think you did?" Anne asked.

"Yes, don't knock them until you try them. They're Alicia's invention." A young woman with a purple mohawk and a pierced nose smiled at them.

"She owns the local co-op at Seven Corners. Didn't picture her as a businesswoman, did you?" Jane said, liking the surprised look on Anne's face.

Bel clicked on reggae tunes. Some of the women danced, others ate, still others discussed serious politics. Anne and Fiona stood back rather stunned by the array of womankind gathered.

"This isn't anything like I expected," Anne told

Fiona as they both ate the strange but good tacos, drinking cold beer discreetly disguised in paper cups.

"Me either," Fiona said, suddenly glad that Anne was there. She felt extremely out of place.

"Where's Louise?"

Fiona rolled her eyes.

"This isn't her kind of party," Anne said.

"Not exactly. She did say she'd set bail if we got arrested."

"That was awfully nice. Are you two doing all right?" Anne asked.

Fiona looked puzzled. Had the rumor mill gotten as far as Anne, or did she know something Fiona didn't?

"Why do you ask? Have you talked to Louise recently?"

"You're just like your sister. Answer a question with a question. No, I haven't. I heard about the ovary incident. I was the one who knocked it off the desk in the first place. I would have liked to see her face when she stepped on it."

Fiona smiled. "It was rather humorous."

Adrienne snapped a picture of the both of them.

Fiona smiled.

"Pity she didn't get a picture of Louise with the ovary," Anne said, studying Fiona as she watched Adrienne, thinking this was all getting rather complicated. Who's worse, she wondered, the woman who chases the married woman or the married woman who allows herself to be seduced? It seems everyone loses. Anne quickly finished her beer.

"Can I get you another?" Fiona offered.

"Sure," Anne said.

Getting tanked seemed to be Anne's new pastime.

She wanted to drink and drink until thoughts of Jane stopped flitting about her head. She knew the only way that was going to happen was when she lay in Jane's arms, feeling herself inside, making Jane come again and again. Until that moment she would never be free. But would she be free or more caught than ever? She had a feeling it would be the latter.

Jane came dashing by, smiled, grabbed her hand, and swung her into the crowd of dancing women. Anne melted into Jane's eyes.

Claudette watched. She lit a cigarette and walked off in the direction of the capitol. Adrienne watched her go thinking she should go with her and give her a shoulder. But she saw Fiona getting a beer and couldn't resist.

"Are you having a good time?"

"I am," Fiona said.

"Good," Adrienne said, gazing deep into her eyes. "Will you come dance with me?"

"I'd love to."

Their eyes locked, asking and answering everything. Adrienne took her hand.

At the appointed hour the Defenders, twenty-five in total, descended on the capitol. They would have to be quick. But there was advantage in their numbers. The women, each armed with two jars, could do a lot. They sent Sarah in to distract the security guard. She put on her best dumb-girl act and strolled in. She kept him out of sight while the Defenders littered the steps of the capitol with oozy gel and feminine body parts.

Sarah stayed at her post until the ruckus of Benton Peugh, his entourage, and various members of the press came streaming out of the capitol. The Defenders formed a line, holding hands and singing old freedom tunes in surprising unison. Sarah took Mary's hand and squeezed it and then just as impetuously kissed her lightly on the cheek. Mary looked over utterly surprised. Sarah took her face gently in her hands and kissed her.

"Sarah!" Mary said.

"I can't help it. You're all I ever think of, and if you don't take me to bed soon I'll die. I'll simply die."

Mary kissed her back. Their ardent embrace was disrupted by the screeches of several female newscasters and the resounding thud of Benton Peugh crashing down into a sea of ovaries. Adrienne wildly snapped photos. Jane envisioned the evening news. It would be absolutely stunning.

Jane moved closer. "Shit, I think he broke his arm."

It did appear broken, sitting at a weird angle as he clutched it to his chest.

"He wasn't supposed to break his arm. Covered in shit is okay, but the arm . . ." Jane murmured.

"Jane!" Fiona said, coming up behind him.

"I can't help it he's a klutz," Jane replied.

"Oh shit, here comes the police," Fiona said, feeling panic flood her body.

"It's okay, Sis, nothing more than a misdemeanor. I checked."

"Officer Reilly, how nice to see you again," Jane said.

The large police officer with dark eyes and thick hair held his hat and only shook his head. He liked Jane. Thought she had guts and too much brain.

He smiled. "Should've figured you'd be behind this. So what's the stuff?"

"I suppose you need to know that for the ticket, eh?"

"I like to be complete."

"Ovaries, and other sundry feminine parts."

"Hmm . . ." Officer Reilly said, marking it down on the ticket.

"We should have brought the Xerox machine for you, and then you could just fill in the blanks," Jane said.

"You're always so thoughtful, Jane," Officer Reilly replied.

"Hey, you've never met my sister. Fiona, this is Officer Reilly."

Fiona looked mortified.

"It's her first time, eh, Jane?"

"That it is."

"And how do you spell your name, miss?"

Louise switched on the news. Sure enough, there they were getting tickets, the steps covered in yuck, and Benton Peugh being asked if he was going to file civil charges for his broken appendage. She saw Fiona standing next to Adrienne, and something in the pit of her stomach jumped. An alarm of sorts that something wasn't quite right.

* * * * *

Back at the office the Defenders proudly pinned their citations to the Wall of Triumph, as they called it, where all the newspaper articles, flyers, citations, bail posted, and other sundry items were placed. The wall was a montage of events, a calendar of moments. Fiona smiled as she placed hers next to Adrienne's. Sarah put hers next to Mary's. Mary squeezed her hand. She didn't understand it, but she knew tonight would be the first of many that she would sleep with the woman she loved nestled in her arms.

The party started all over again with more women joining them. When the news kicked on, everyone stopped and huddled around the television. Shouts and cheers erupted as the Defenders saw their handiwork.

"I couldn't have done it better myself," Jane said, admiring the staging. "They captured it beautifully."

Fiona wondered if Louise had condescended to watch them. She hadn't quite given Fiona her blessing in going, but she had wished her well, kissed her good-bye, and given her an odd look of longing and forgiveness. And then she said, "Please remember, no matter what happens I always love you, will always love you," as if she knew something, as if she knew Fiona had spent time with the computer buddy. If only they could talk, but somehow they were past that.

Fiona went upstairs to call. She had to know what Louise was feeling this very moment. She would ask her if she had seen them on the news. She sat on the corner of her desk and called home. She had to know where they stood. Everything hinged on this moment. Sink or swim right now, Fiona thought as the phone rang, one, two, three, four times, then the voice

163

messaging picked up, meaning the line was being used. Louise said she'd be home. The line was busy, busy talking, typing, or whatever the two of them did. Fiona cursed technology. So you can fuck online now. It was sick. She held the phone to her chest.

Adrienne walked in.

"Are you all right?"

"Yes. I just needed to make a phone call."

Adrienne walked toward her. "Thanks for coming tonight."

"It was fun, and I'm glad I did."

"Are you in trouble?"

"Trouble?"

"At home," Adrienne said, taking the phone from Fiona and setting it down.

"I don't think so. It appears that Louise is keeping herself busy these days."

"And what about you?" Adrienne said, brushing a stray lock of hair from Fiona's face. Their eyes locked. Adrienne was standing very close. Fiona could feel her breath, smell her skin. She felt her own breath quicken, her heartbeat echo in her chest.

"Adrienne . . ."

Adrienne put her hands on Fiona's shoulders, studying her face, looking deep into her eyes, searching. Fiona felt her knuckles go white as her hands tightened on the edge of the desk.

"I won't hurt you, and I wouldn't do anything you didn't want," Adrienne said, sliding her hands down Fiona's arms, her touch making them both flush, "but you have to say, you have to be the one."

Fiona stayed quiet, thinking, leaping from side to side, plucking petals from the flower of desire — I want, I shouldn't want — until the image in her head revealed the petals strewn about her feet. It seemed an eternity. A decision of such consequence that held all the joy and misery that falling in love brings.

"I'm scared. I'm so scared."

Adrienne pulled her close, her arms wrapped around Fiona's neck, her face nestled in the crook of Fiona's neck. If this was as close as she got, then this was the edge of paradise. And if this was all she got, she was still a happy woman.

Fiona pulled away and looked at her. "I want, I want things that shouldn't be but I can't help how I feel, the things I feel . . ." She put her hands on Adrienne's face and softly kissed her, kissed her again deeper, reaching for her. Adrienne pulled the tie from her hair, letting it fall. So many nights she dreamed of doing that, of seeing Fiona's dark hair cascade about her shoulders, of kissing her neck and feeling her hands stroke her strong back, of feeling the muscles tense and relax, of feeling herself being pulled close, of her body being wrapped around by Fiona's long legs.

It was happening. Then both of them were on the desk, stuff was falling, being pushed everywhere. Undoing Fiona's blouse, finding her breast with her tongue, feeling her own shirt being pulled off, and pants and bras and shirts somehow coming off, feeling Fiona lift her cunt to her face. And then her tongue inside. Adrienne arched her back.

Fiona let her hands run the length of Adrienne's body, bringing them to rest on her hips, then slipping one hand underneath and sliding a finger inside, still gliding her tongue between the pink folds, feeling Adrienne rocking back and forth until she softly cried out. Sliding her body down the length of Fiona's. Coming to rest at lips, looking deep into her eyes, kissing her gently, murmuring sounds of want.

The weight of Adrienne's slim body on her own felt electric. Fiona thought when Adrienne touched her she'd have to try hard not to come that very moment. Adrienne took her time, kissing Fiona's neck, then her breasts, her hipbones, her toes, the insides of her thighs. And then her tongue, gently at first and then harder, thrust inside her. Fingers filled her.

Adrienne stood, pulling Fiona to the edge of the desk. Fiona's legs were wrapped around Adrienne, pulling closer, rocking slowly. Fiona felt soft lips on her neck. Then Adrienne moved with more intensity, grinding, pulling them together tight, like two for a brief moment becoming one, and quivering, feeling her whole body convulse. Fiona felt limp in Adrienne's arms.

"I've never made love there before," Fiona said.

Adrienne ran her fingers through Fiona's hair. Looking at her intensely she asked, "Are you all right?"

Fiona blushed at the care and concern with which Adrienne spoke. "I'm wonderful. Just hold me."

They crossed the room and lay naked on the couch, watching the streetlight dance across the darkened room. Through the open window they could hear the noises from the party and the street below. They were silent, stroking each other's skin, listening to heartbeats and breathing, and then making love again, slower this time, watching each other's face and then coming together, as if they were meant to make love, meant to quiver and fall at the same time, meant to lie sweating and breathless in one another's arms.

And then clunk, clunk, the even thud of someone's boots on the stairs.

"Oh shit!" Adrienne said, getting up. She grabbed Fiona's shirt and threw it to her. They both scrambled to get dressed.

"I shouldn't be here," Adrienne said, frantically looking for a place to hide.

"Here," Fiona said, positioning her by the desk. "Sit here."

Adrienne slunk down by the desk. Unless someone sat at the desk she wouldn't be seen. Fiona touched her cheek and smiled.

Jane walked in. "There you are. I wondered where you got off to."

"I came up to call home."

"Is everything okay?"

"I don't know. I couldn't get through."

Jane looked around at the mess on the floor and then at Fiona, who appeared slightly disheveled. Maybe it was the way her blouse was buttoned. One button off, and it gave the whole thing away.

"Let me guess: You were cleaning up your office," Jane said, kicking the stapler that was lying on the floor.

"Something like that," Fiona said.

"Don't get into trouble," Jane said, tugging at Fiona's blouse.

Fiona blushed. "I won't. I should be heading out soon anyway."

"I'll walk you out."

"Let me get my stuff together, and I'll meet you downstairs."

"I'll wait."

"Jane, please."

"Okay," Jane said, smiling, knowing now that Fiona's lover was in the room. Fifty bucks it was Adrienne, fucking better be Adrienne, Jane thought.

Fiona sank down on the couch. "I'm sorry."

"Don't be. Don't ever be sorry," Adrienne said.

Fiona took her in her arms. "You deserve better than this."

"Have dinner with me tomorrow. I'll cook. I just want you all to myself for an evening. Can you arrange it?"

"I'm yours."

Nine

"We should send him flowers," Jane said.

"Who?" Mary asked.

"Benton Peugh. After all, we did facilitate his breaking his arm."

"True. But this seems a little out of character for you."

"Why?"

"Aren't you the one that threw the flowers out the window?" Mary said.

"Yes."

"What makes you think he won't do the same thing?"

"It doesn't matter," Jane said.

"Why doesn't it matter?"

"Because I knew she sent the flowers. It was my prerogative to do whatever with them."

"So her end was still achieved."

"Exactly."

"What kind?" Mary asked, getting out the yellow pages and thumbing through for florists. Maybe she'd send Sarah a dozen red roses while she was at it.

"Lilies, I think. White lilies," Jane replied.

Fiona woke with a snap. She'd been dreaming, but she couldn't grasp it. She looked over at Louise, who was sleeping peacefully. She remembered creeping into bed late last night, Louise murmuring and then rolling over, her opening one sleepy eye, smiling briefly, and then drifting back to unconsciousness. Fiona lay awake, staring at her and thinking back over the night. Even something as commonplace as driving home suddenly seemed foreign, as if she wasn't living her own life and was instead watching someone else's. Pulling up in the driveway, washing her face, changing into a T-shirt, getting in bed, pretending to be something she now knew she wasn't: a faithful lover. But in all this unraveling drama, she didn't see herself telling Louise either. It wasn't something Louise needed to know. Whether they made it or not, knowing she'd slept with Adrienne would only take them places they didn't need to go. The infidelity wasn't about them; it was about her and whatever it was that had dragged her this far away from Louise. Was that why Louise hadn't told her about cybersex?

"I hate it when I can't answer my own questions," Fiona murmured softly. She got up to shower.

Fiona stood with her eyes closed, feeling the hot water stream down her body. Making love on a desktop had left her sore. She heard the shower door click open. She looked over, surprised. Louise smiled, ran her hand across Fiona's cheek and kissed her softly on the mouth, then her neck, her torso, until she was kneeling, taking Fiona in her mouth. Fiona ran her hands through Louise's hair, stroking her head, feeling herself cry out, hearing her cry echo against the shower walls. She brought Louise to her, slipping her hand between Louise's legs, pulling her close, holding her, going deeper, feeling Louise's back go taut as she gasped in Fiona's ear.

"Good morning," Fiona whispered.

"Hmm . . . wonderful morning," Louise replied.

"We're going to run out of hot water soon," Fiona said, handing Louise the soap. Louise lathered it and washed Fiona.

"I think I need to take more vitamins," Fiona said, as she lay looking at the towel-strewn floor and at Louise between her legs, her head on Fiona's stomach.

Louise came up and snuggled close. "I don't know about vitamins, but I'm famished. Let's go out for breakfast."

"Can you take the morning off?"

"I shouldn't, but I'm going to."

Fiona looked deep in Louise's eyes, held her face in her hands.

"What's wrong?" Louise asked, feeling more vulnerable than she had ever felt in her entire life.

"Where have you been?"

"What do you mean?" Louise asked nervously.

"This you, the one here this morning."

"Away, I sent her away when I needed her most. Now let's go eat," Louise said, scrambling out of bed.

"Louise?"

"Yes?"

"I love you."

"Ditto."

That was her morning, this was her night, standing beneath the billowing tents of the Farmer's Market, picking out roma tomatoes, and looking up to see Adrienne watching her from the across the stands with such a look of love it frightened Fiona. Utter love gushed from Adrienne's pores, was exhaled in every breath, clouding her eyes. Fiona stared back, mesmerized by the passion, forgetting everything else, forgetting even herself. She walked over to where Adrienne stood in front of the gleaming purple eggplants and let her hand slide into Adrienne's. She picked up an eggplant, holding it neatly in her palm, as if balancing the golden orb of perpetual happiness.

"This is a good one. Shall we take it?"

"Hmm . . ." Adrienne replied, thinking, How many more minutes will I have to endure before I hold you in my arms again?

They made it through dinner, barely. Fiona was ready to seduce Adrienne on the dinner table. Neither of them talked much over dinner, as if words seemed too trite to explain what was happening. Fiona kept thinking about Coleridge's willing suspension of disbelief, that this was happening and not happening at the same time, a charming of the heart and soul that the mind kept trying to interject with reason, trying to scream out, Look at what you're doing. Fiona forgot everything and simply dove into Adrienne's eyes and waited to drown in her lovely arms.

When Adrienne ran a bath and lit candles, Fiona followed her faith in desire with perfectly amoral behavior, thinking, I believe in this moment, I need no others. Would she look back on it and regret it? It didn't matter. In one day her whole life had turned upside down, and she sailed rudderless across her own reality.

Adrienne teased and cajoled her through the bath, wanting to make her come but slipping away at the right moment until Fiona thought she'd die from the mere thought of orgasm. But once in bed, her legs wrapped around Adrienne, she let go such a primordial scream of delight, it surprised them both. Adrienne was taking her places she'd never been. She felt like a teenager feeling lust for the first time, like a maiden aunt being fucked for all the years she'd abstained rolled into one sticky sweet mess of come, all over her, all over Adrienne, all over the sheets.

Later she lay on the couch at home unable to sleep, thinking she'd walked into her house, kissed her wife good night, held her and murmured I love you with perfect ease. While hours before she'd been ardently fucking someone else, fucking without constraint, without rules, without thought, without the promise of waking up together and having coffee. Fucking for the first time, for the last, and for times in between. Careening down a hill recklessly smiling with passion and laughter. How did this work? she asked herself, and no answer came to mind.

She felt like Louise when she asked those questions. Questions she'd never asked before, never had to ask. How does it work? Not like a Cuisinart, or a ninety-dollar corkscrew or a money market account. It worked like an addiction, an obsession, a fetish, and any other word that took a lover from the safe zone of monogamy to the fringes of insanity. She was no longer in control of her body, her mind, or her spirit. They'd been pirated, and she waited willingly for the next voyage.

"Claudette, it's not like that," Jane said, studying the photographs Adrienne had pinned up on the wall. She was getting good. Now these were book material, Jane thought. Maybe Anne wasn't so far off when she suggested doing a book on the Defenders, maybe it was time to branch out a little.

"Then tell me what it's like," Claudette demanded, suddenly feeling like her father when faced with her mother's infidelities. This wasn't supposed to be happening. They'd both slept with other people, and they always came back from these casual liaisons with little damage, oftentimes with nothing more than a few laughs and a few new positions. It was like trying a new flavor of ice cream only to discover you liked your old favorite best. They'd never found anyone else they liked better than each other. But this time was different.

"What do you want to know? Am I fucking her? No."

"I wouldn't care if you were fucking her, it's the falling in love part that scares me. Are you falling in love with her?"

Their eyes met. Jane wished she could get down on her knees and swear she wasn't in love. Her hesitation said everything. Claudette turned away. She could feel tears. She left.

Jane slumped to the floor, thinking, I don't know what I feel anymore, but I don't want to lose you. And then she wondered which *you* she was referring to. She put on her Rollerblades and went skating downtown. She was beginning to understand why Fiona went running. She ended up at her mother's front porch.

"Does obsession run in our family?" Jane asked, before her mother had a chance to say hello.

Hazel set her glass of iced tea down and rocked slowly in the swing on the porch. She patted the cushion.

"Come sit. Let me tell you a story."

She told her the story of the Italian professor, thinking it was time she told someone. She didn't know then that she was telling the wrong daughter.

"So obsession does run in the family," Jane said, taking her mother's hand.

"I think it's a universal construct, dear. Now tell me, what is going on with Fiona? She won't say, and I can't help but worry. There is something, isn't there?"

"Yes."

As Jane rolled off, Hazel thought, I wish Fiona would confide in me as Jane does. I could help if she'd let me. But Fiona is like me. She'll suffer in her own private hell, holding herself solely responsible for everything that has gone wrong, unable to share because that would mean opening up, being vulnerable, admitting to imperfection. Hazel knew where she got this. Heredity could definitely be a curse.

Ten

"Hello, darling. Did you miss me?" Margo said, as she flounced in looking incredibly tanned and sporting a lot of new gold jewelry of intricate design. She had just gotten back from Morocco.

Fiona took one look at her and spilled the beans. "I slept with Adrienne." They both looked shocked that she said it. Fiona didn't know why she blurted it out.

"What a busy little beaver you've become."

Fiona laughed and gave her a hug. "You weren't

here when I needed you most, and now look what I've gone and done."

"Something marvelous, I'd say."

"What am I going to do?"

"Enjoy yourself. I know that's a foreign concept for you, but try it, you might find that you like it."

"I mean about guilt, remorse, penitence, and forgiveness."

"Darling, leave off the Catholic bullshit and let's go have a drink. I'm in dire need of a gimlet. And then after I've convinced you of the beauty of this new experience I shall tell you about the simply stunning archeologist I met. I still quiver thinking about her," Margo said.

"You know, the funny part is that I don't feel guilty. I feel almost amoral. I feel that I'm living two separate lives on the same plane."

"Have you been reading Einstein again?" Margo said, putting her hand on her hip and raising her eyebrow.

"No."

"Hmm . . . my only advice to you is to not overprocess the thing. Is she good in bed?"

Fiona was affronted and then she smiled. "Incredible."

"Figures."

"You know what they say about women with strange hairdos."

"No, tell me," Margo said.

"Drink first."

* * * * *

178

"Are you sure you want to do this?" Margo asked, as she dropped Fiona at her mother's.

"I need to talk to her," Fiona said, holding the door handle of Margo's Lexus for a moment longer than she should have.

"Why not wait until your four gimlets have worn off?"

"The gimlets are the only reason I'm here," Fiona said, opening the door, thinking it was now or never.

"All right. I wouldn't expect her to be sympathetic."

"Why?"

"Because straight people, especially if they're our parents, expect perfect moral behavior."

"We're already deviant."

"No excuse."

"Wish me luck."

"You'll need more than that."

"I'll call you," Fiona said.

Hazel was out back watering her flowers with the heavy brass watering can that had been Charles's. She always felt close to him whenever she was in the garden.

"Well, hello, darling. How are you?" Hazel said, giving Fiona a hug and smelling alcohol. Something serious was up, and Hazel knew what.

"Mom . . ."

"Look, darling, how well the snowdrops and asters are doing. Your father would be proud. I do miss him.

And look at how beautifully the bulb garden is doing. Not quite Holland, but definitely full looking," Hazel said, pointing to the bright red tulips.

"Mom, my life is falling apart right now, and I don't give a damn about the garden."

"Fiona, you needn't be rude. It's not my fault you slept with Adrienne."

"How did you know?"

Hazel bit her lip.

"Jane told you, didn't she? How does she know? How can she have the audacity to think that she can tell you something she can't for certain know herself?"

"Fiona, wait!" Hazel said, going after her.

Fiona turned. "No, I came for your help only to discover the duplicity of my own family."

Hazel called to warn Jane. She wasn't in the office, but Mary promised to relay the message.

Fiona locked herself in the office and cried. She'd never felt so confused, sad, angry, and disappointed in her entire life. If this was what passion was all about, perhaps stasis was better. She thought back to the days when she longed for something incredible to happen, for someone to walk into her life and make her feel special, to whisper stupid little vanities like she loved Fiona's body, or that Fiona had incredible eyes, or that she loved how she felt when Fiona was moving inside her. And now all that was happening with Adrienne, and yet she had begun to crave the days of normalcy, days when she didn't feel that she was endlessly walking a tightrope between two women, relishing the thrill yet fearful of the fall.

Jane knocked on the door.

"Go away."

"Fiona, come on. This isn't very grown-up, you know."

"I don't care to be grown-up. Besides, tattling isn't grown-up either."

"I don't understand what the big deal is," Jane said.

"It may not be a big deal to you, but it's a very big deal to me. And I'd like to know how you got your information."

"Isn't she everything you imagined?" Jane said.

"What's that supposed to mean? I suppose you slept with her too. Did you tell Mom that?"

"I don't feel the need to confess," Jane said.

"So you did sleep with her. What does she have, a penchant for sisters?"

"Fiona, open this fucking door right now. I refuse to argue with you this way."

"And I refuse to open it. Now go away."

"I'm not going away until you talk to me properly."

"As you wish," Fiona said. She could hear Jane thump down in front of the door. She quietly opened the window and climbed down the fire escape.

Adrienne went to find Jane at Mary's insistence.

"What are you doing?" Adrienne asked when she found Jane waiting outside Fiona's office.

"Waiting for Fiona to open the door," Jane said, chewing on her cuticles.

"She's gone."

"What do you mean?" Jane asked, getting up.

"She drove the Beemer today, right?"

"Yes."

"Well, it's gone and the fire escape ladder is hanging down. Three guesses."

"Shit!"

"Why are you fighting?"

"She's mad at me for telling Mom that you two were sleeping together."

"What!" Adrienne said, feeling the pit of her stomach drop to the floor.

"It's not a big deal, Adrienne."

"Oh my god. How could you have done this? Fiona probably thinks I told you. How do you know, anyway?"

"The rough-and-tumble on the desktop the night of the demonstration. I'm not blind."

"Why did you tell your mother?"

"She asked, and I didn't think Fiona would ever have the balls to tell her. I didn't want her to worry."

"What am I going to do?" Adrienne said, feeling panic set in.

"About what?" Jane asked, confusion curdling her features.

"About Fiona."

"Enjoy her while you can."

"What's that supposed to mean?"

"Adrienne . . . think about it. Fiona is not just a little playmate, and you're not as grown-up as you think."

"Fuck you," Adrienne said, taking a last hard look at Jane and leaving.

"Three out of three. Jesus, somebody get me a bat

so I can knock myself silly," Jane said, banging her head against the door.

Jane dialed the condo number and waited for the ring. Anne answered.

"Can you come down?"

"I have a better idea. Why don't you come up?" Anne teased.

"No. I'm serious. You need to come down."

"All right."

Jane watched her come across the lobby. She looked so small and vulnerable dressed in a T-shirt, untucked, a pair of khaki shorts, and no shoes. Her hair was messy, as if she might have been napping on the couch, relaxing on a Sunday afternoon. Jane felt an overwhelming desire to hold and kiss her, to whisper I'm in love with you and I can't help it. Instead, she had come to say good-bye.

Anne smiled. "This is a pleasant surprise."

Jane stood looking at her.

"What's wrong?"

Jane took her hand and ran it down the side of Anne's face. Anne leaned toward her, closing her eyes. She opened them and looked at Jane.

"I can't see you anymore," Jane said, hurt and confusion riding across her face.

"Jane . . ." Anne cried out after her, but Jane was already halfway down the street, skating as hard as she could. Anne sat on the curb and felt a cold, hard lump form in her chest. She felt pain, as if something had been plucked from her by the root.

A half hour later the security guard came out.

"Are you all right, Ms. Beaumont?"

Anne got up quickly. Any other day she would have politely lied.

"No, I'm not all right."

She walked inside.

"Darling, are you home?" Louise called out.

Fiona was in the bath, with a bottle of merlot. She'd been crying, and Louise would know it.

Louise found her in the bathroom.

"Can I come in?" Louise asked, standing in the doorway.

"Sure."

Louise sat on the toilet, looking horribly guilty despite her best attempt to the contrary. "What's wrong?" she asked, trying to brace herself for the proverbial other shoe to drop.

"Bad day," Fiona replied, studying the soap dish with acute attention.

"What happened?" Louise asked, trying desperately to keep the rising panic from her voice.

Fiona looked at her and burst into tears.

Louise held her while she sobbed.

Louise put Fiona to bed and stroked her head, watching her sleep. They never talked about it, each leaving the other to whatever conclusions she had drawn. All they knew for certain was that it was over.

Having reached the end of destruction, they could start over.

In the morning when Fiona awoke, Louise brought her coffee and toast in bed. She looked at her shyly.

"I'm sorry," Louise said.

"Me too. Can we try again?" Fiona asked, wanting it more than she could have ever imagined.

"Do you want to?" Louise asked, feeling more sorry than she ever thought possible and swearing to herself she would never hurt Fiona like this again.

"Very much."

"Hold me," Louise said.

Adrienne and Claudette sat in the back alley behind the Gay Nineties off Hennepin, sharing a bottle of cheap wine and smoking cigarettes. They knew no one would find them there. No one seeks those who live in alleys trying to find the lost pieces of themselves.

"I can't believe I let myself get this far," Adrienne said, lighting another cigarette.

"But isn't that what love is, the letting yourself go?" Claudette said, feeling drunk and philosophical in the same instance.

"But why do we even want love when it always ends up in letting go?"

"Not all love is letting go."

"Are you letting go?" Adrienne asked, staring at her hard.

"I have to. Jane let go when she fell for another," Claudette replied. She took a long swig off the bottle, hoping it would squelch any further philosophical moments.

"Has she slept with Anne?"

"She says she hasn't," Claudette said, pursing her lips in obvious distaste. She still couldn't believe Jane was selling out to that woman.

"Do you believe her?"

"Yes."

"Then you don't have to end it," Adrienne said brightly.

"This isn't about sex," Claudette said, disdainfully.

"What's it about then?" Adrienne asked, utterly confused.

"Finding your soul mate."

"Jane isn't your soul mate? I thought that was how it worked, how you two could play around and still keep coming back to each other."

"She is mine, but I'm obviously not hers. Not anymore."

"How can we have soul mates if she's yours but you're not hers?" Adrienne asked.

"Because sometimes Fate and Destiny don't smile at one another; they hurl objects and scream nasty words. Losing your soul mate is the result."

"So you're saying you're the casualty of an argument."

"It's better to have known love and lost than never to have known love at all," Claudette said.

"You're sounding maudlin," Adrienne stated flatly.

"And what are you?"

"A fool," Adrienne said, feeling tears build up.

"Let's go take a bath," Claudette said, wiping Adrienne's tears with the corner of her shirt.

"Together?"

"Yes."

"A baptism?" Adrienne asked, wiping her snotty nose on her sleeve.

"Precisely," Claudette said, taking the last swig of the bottle, standing up with obvious difficulty, and throwing it against the brick wall.

They smiled at each other as the bottle crashed into the wall.

Jane stood in the bathroom door with tears running down her face.

Claudette looked at her. "Go away."

Jane knelt down next to them, holding them together. She kissed their wet foreheads.

"I will always love you."

"I know," Claudette said, doing her best not to cry.

Jane walked the streets until dawn, thinking about when Anne had told her if she was her girlfriend she would never need to stray, never feel the need, never know another want. She had laughed. Pretty sure of yourself, aren't you. When you find your other, Jane, there isn't room for anyone else, Anne had told her. She was cold and tired when she reached Anne's door. She buzzed.

"Yes," Anne answered groggily.

"Can I come up? I need to see you."

"Jane?"

"Yes."

Anne opened the door. Every nerve in her body felt

tight and abused. She knew her eyes were red and that she looked like shit.

"You look tired," Anne said.

"I've been up all night," Jane said, realizing it had probably been more like a few days. Somewhere she had lost count. She wasn't sure anymore where she was supposed to be sleeping, which made getting some sleep difficult. She guessed that was why she was here.

"You've been crying," Jane replied.

"I have," Anne said, not looking at Jane. She felt too raw and out of control to meet her gaze.

"Why?"

"Because I've never been in love before," Anne said, shoving her hands in her pockets when she really wanted to take Jane in her arms.

"I need to lie down," Jane said, looking drawn.

Anne put her to bed and waited, not knowing what was coming. She didn't dare hope.

Hours later when Jane awoke, she wrapped a sheet around herself and went to find Anne in the living room. She was sleeping on the couch. She looked small and vulnerable, like a child. Jane knew from that moment there was no returning to the safe zone of ambivalent love affairs. This was hook, line, sinker, and big fish. It wasn't a Sunday afternoon picnic where promises are made and subsequently broken when the reality of Monday creeps in. Jane touched her Anne's cheek, half wondering if she would be seared at the touch for being a heretic in the religion of love for so long. But was she really ready to become an acolyte?

"I love you," Jane said, trying not to tremble.

Anne sat up slowly and rubbed her eyes, wondering if she was dreaming. She smiled when she realized she was actually conscious and Jane was standing in front of her, naked except for a sheet, telling her she loved her.

"I'm not dreaming?" she teased.

"Hold me, please," Jane said, still trembling.

Anne pulled Jane to her, whispering, "I have never longed for those words. I've always feared them."

Jane kissed her slowly.

"Do you fear them now?" Jane asked, looking intently in her eyes.

"No," Anne said, running her hands across Jane's shoulders, the sheet dropping to the floor. She kissed her bare shoulders, running her hands gently across Jane's back and butt, pulling her closer, then kneeling, kissing her stomach. Jane ran her fingers through Anne's hair. Anne took her into her mouth. Jane closed her eyes, letting sensation take hold. She put her hand on the side of the couch for support. She felt herself come, felt Anne's firm hands caressing the back of her thighs. Anne stood and nestled her face in the crook of Jane's neck.

"Take me to bed," she said.

Jane obeyed. She took her hand and led her to the bedroom. They stood by the side of the bed, looked at its massive white fluffiness, and then at each other. Anne smiled.

"It's not like we've never done this before," she teased.

"This is different," Jane said, seriousness clouding her face. She took Anne's face in her hands and gently kissed her forehead. Jane lifted her shirt over her head slowly, finding herself quivering with anticipation at seeing her lover's body for the first time. Jane hadn't quivered over anyone since she was in the fifth grade and Laura Dempson french-kissed her behind the portables.

Anne let her shorts fall to the ground and pulled Jane with her to the bed. Jane lowered herself on top of Anne, their nipples and cunts fitting together perfectly. Jane kissed Anne and took her hands and lifted them above her head, effectively pinning her to the bed. Jane read the moment of panic in Anne's eyes.

She kissed her again softly and whispered, "I would never hurt you."

Anne nodded and relaxed while Jane performed the most erotic act of full body tribadism, from the top of her head to the tip of her toes, she had ever experienced. It was as if Jane's cunt danced all over her body. Jane made love to her nipples, her clit, and then seriously finger-fucked her. Sweaty and highly overstimulated, Anne raised her head to look at her new lover. She knew from that moment forward she was a slave to her own lust and her partner's talents.

"My god, Jane," Anne said, rolling up on her elbow. She traced the line of sweat that ran between Jane's breasts.

"Have you ever noticed how people evoke God a lot during sex?" Jane said, smiling up at Anne.

Anne smiled back and neatly inserted her knee between Jane's legs. The next words out of Jane's

mouth had nothing to do with God and were not
rhetorically correct in any known language.

Fiona stayed away from the office for a few days.
She went running, trying to clear her head. Her
mother called several times and then gave up. Hazel
knew her daughter would come around when she was
ready. Louise, picking up on the same vibe, gave her
space. Fiona kept thinking, If only they had behaved
like this before, none of this would have happened.
Now they had hurt themselves and others. It was the
others Fiona was currently worried about. She didn't
know how she was going to face Adrienne.

How was she going to say, I'm sorry I let you walk
into my life, I'm sorry I let you touch me that way?
Fiona kept replaying the last time they had been
together, a wonderful clandestine rendezvous. They
had made love all afternoon, watching the sky grow
dimmer, the hot afternoon fade, the light splash across
their bodies. Fiona on her stomach, Adrienne on top
of her, her breasts soft and warm against Fiona's
back, whispering love things, feeling inside her, kissing
her neck. It was a setting Fiona would never forget.

This remembering, this etching for posterity, must
have been linked to her knowing their love affair was
a fleeting thing. Could she honestly say she meant for
the two of them to form a union, to buy a house with
the white picket fence? She'd like to say she hadn't
known, that she was open to the option. But she did
know, and that was why she had memorized every
kiss, every look, every touch. She had to; this was an

affair of brevity, and remembrances were all either of them would ever have.

Jane kissed the back of Anne's neck. The smell of lavender soap lingered on her skin.

"I don't think I've had clothes on for quite some time," Jane said, smiling.

"At least we finally got around to taking a bath. I think we were starting to smell," Anne replied.

Jane went to find a T-shirt.

"Jane . . ." Anne called out.

"Yes?" Jane asked, popping her head back in the bathroom.

"I don't think I've ever been this happy," Anne said, her face a mixture of glee and perplexity.

"And you're frightened . . ."

"Petrified."

Jane held her. "Don't be. Now finish up and I'll make you one of my favorite omelets, and if it's not your favorite at least have the common decency to fake it."

"What if I told you I didn't like eggs?" Anne teased.

"You'd eat them because you love me."

"I do."

"Remember those two words, you might need them someday."

Anne looked at herself in the mirror. She looked different. She looked like a woman in love. She remembered lying in bed next to Jane, two women alone in the world, staring into each other's eyes as if they were touching souls, then touching bodies, then making love again. Anne had never been consumed like this before, and it made her fearful. If Jane left she would surely die. All those things she'd read about love — the intensity of love, the drive of love, the things it got people to do. Anne had always thought it melodrama, words for fools and notions for the weak minded. Now, she believed.

Jane answered the door. Holly looked surprised.

"Where's Anne?"

"I've got her tied to the bed at the moment. Would you like me to go get her?"

Holly was taken aback. With someone like Jane, anything was possible. She was concerned about Anne. No one had seen her for a week. She hadn't returned any of her phone calls at home, and mail and messages had piled up at her office. It was as if she had disappeared from the face of the planet.

Anne came out of the bedroom. "Holly, how are you?" she said, obviously surprised.

"I should ask the same of you. I came to see if you'd been abducted by aliens. People are beginning to worry about you."

Jane smiled from behind the kitchen bar where she was chopping up vegetables.

"You don't count as an alien," Anne said, knowing what Jane was thinking.

"Alternate life form?" Jane queried.

"Perhaps."

"So you're all right?" Holly asked.

"Don't I look all right?" Anne asked.

"Lesbian hyperanalyzation, answer a question with a question," Jane said.

"I believe that's my rhetoric, young lady," Anne said.

"What is going on?" Holly asked. "Are you two an item now or what?"

"I'll be the toothpaste and you be the soap," Jane said.

"Yes, in the supermarket of life," Anne replied. They both laughed.

"I think you two have been cooped up a little too long. You should go out for a walk or something," Holly said.

"She's probably right, you know," Jane said.

"I know. But I'm afraid if I let you out of my sight you won't come back."

"I wouldn't worry about that. I'm just as infatuated with you as you are with me," Jane said.

"See there. Everything is fine. Come to work tomorrow. Jane's not going to vaporize if you're not with her for a few hours. I really need your help," Holly said.

"I know. I'm sorry," Anne replied, feeling not one pang of guilt though she knew she should. At the moment the mere suggestion of allowing real life to enter her forest of delight seemed horribly distasteful. Holly was looking suspiciously like a bright yellow bulldozer about to destroy paradise.

"Tomorrow?" Holly said.

"Tomorrow," Anne swore halfheartedly.

"Jane?" Holly said.

"I'll push her out the door if I have to," Jane promised.

Anne walked Holly out.

In the hall Holly asked, "So you're really all right then?"

"Holly, I'm fine. I'm better than fine. I'm in love." Holly nodded. "Okay then."

194

"Why haven't we been out of this apartment?" Anne asked Jane as she wrapped her arms around her and kissed her cheek softly.

"Because we're scared everything will change once we let the rest of the world in," Jane said, flipping the omelet with expert precision. She'd been a short-order cook more than once.

"Will it?" Anne asked, trying not to be fearful of the answer.

"No, it will make us stronger and better," Jane said, pulling her close and holding her tight, murmuring a litany of *I love you*'s.

Claudette was lying in the middle of the loft apartment she had once shared with someone named Jane. She supposed she should be doing something, but all she could think about was Jane. Adrienne had done her best to keep her occupied until Claudette finally told her she needed some time to think, to sort through things. She was running the course of their relationship through her head, attempting to memorize, blazon forever upon her mind, how they had once been.

It was a difficult fact to realize that subscribing to nonmonogamy had been a mistake, not that it would have kept Jane out of that viperous woman's reach, only that monogamy might have cemented their bond so closely that someone like Anne would never have come between them. Unfortunately, open dating had turned into open season on her heart.

She couldn't say for certain when they decided that they could be together but not together as in *I own you*, which is how they viewed the monogamy of their friends. She remembered telling Jane that she liked her too much to do something as banal as commit to a lifetime, that she didn't want to lose her because they would each become a ball and chain for the other. Jane had laughed wickedly but turned immediately crimson when Claudette asked her if she was still sleeping with the TA in her art history class.

My point being, she told Jane, was that if I try to cage you, you will only hate me later. From that moment forward they took lovers and took each other, sometimes in the same night. What did that make them? Claudette used to think it made them free, it made them defy the status quo and all its petty behaviors.

Now she doubted everything: love, philosophy, and her own personal revolution. Did she really, underneath it all, wish for the normal life, the lesbian version of home on the range, where you didn't get to fuck around with the other cowgirls? Jane was the only other person in the world who understood that in Claudette's mind commitment was more like a prison term than the bars themselves. To her it was her parents' failed marriage over and over again. And she knew she would never be able to go there and not have those same cooped-up feelings she felt when she was a child. Love, to her, was a claustrophobia of the heart.

Eleven

Fiona knocked on Adrienne's door. What had once seemed so familiar was now foreign. They were shy in each other's presence.

"I didn't tell Jane about us," Adrienne blurted.

"I know," Fiona said, avoiding Adrienne's gaze.

"Why did you run away?"

"I needed some time to think."

"About what?"

"Us."

"Has there ever really been an us?" Adrienne said, turning away.

Fiona looked out the window, studying the skyline. There had been a time as she had lain curled up around Adrienne when she hadn't wanted to go home. When she thought she might be able to start over, to leave Louise and her old life behind. But going home, holding Louise, watching her sleep, thinking about life without her, reliving their past, seeing their life now as it evolved into something new and better, she knew where she needed to be. Fiona turned back around.

"I can't see you anymore."

"I know."

"I'm so sorry," Fiona said, pain written across her face.

"So am I," Adrienne replied, trying not cry.

Fiona took one last look at Adrienne and left. She drove home in tears, wishing she had never known Adrienne, wishing she'd never cheated on Louise and longing for an innocence she had too willingly given up.

When Mary finally tore herself away from Sarah and forced her to go to class, she arrived at work to find Adrienne and Claudette drunk at ten in the morning. She had the distinct impression they'd been at it all night.

"It seems everyone is getting laid but us," Claudette said, lighting two cigarettes and handing one to Adrienne.

"Seems like it," Adrienne said. She took a swig of beer and let out a heavy sigh. "So I take it that morning has arrived."

Claudette peeked through the blind. "It appears so. Good thing, because we're almost out of beer."

"What is going on around here?" Mary asked. She hadn't seen Jane in a week, and Fiona was just as infrequent. And now all this drinking.

"Hell has no fury like a woman scorned. We just haven't gotten around to doing anything about it," Claudette said.

"Now's there's one dude who knew his stuff about love. I think Fiona has been reading Sonnet 129," Adrienne said, thinking back to her college days and all the tedious memorization she'd suffered in the quest for the almighty sheepskin.

"I'm not familiar with that one," Claudette replied.

"The falling away of lust once the object has been obtained. Sanity arrives and saves the poor, imperiled soul," Adrienne stated.

Mary sat on the edge of the coffee table, looking the role of the perfect older sister about to give advice.

"You two need to get a grip on yourselves. Maudlin drunkenness is not going to fix anything. Activity will. Now you need to decide what you're going to do."

Claudette and Adrienne made silly faces at each other and burst out laughing.

"I mean it. This has got to stop," Mary said, getting up and putting her hands on her hips.

"She's right. It's time for activity," Adrienne said.

"Uh-huh, let's go get some more beer," Claudette said, getting up and trying to rescue Adrienne from the clutches of the couch.

"Stunning idea," Adrienne said, getting up with some difficulty.

They gave Mary an elaborate bow and exited giggling.

Mary sat at her desk shaking her head. Yeats's "The Second Coming" poem came to mind: "Things fall apart." Smart men, Yeats and Shakespeare, but neither of them fixed anything; they just brought it to the world's attention.

Jane peeked her head in the door. "Are you alone?"

"Yes, Jane, where have you been? Everything is in utter chaos. I need your help," Mary said.

"Bit messy, eh?" Jane said, sticking her hands deep in her pockets and rocking back on her heels.

"More than a bit," Mary replied.

"What's been going on?" Jane asked tentatively.

"Both Fiona and Anne have gone missing, and we need them to get this book thing for the Defenders going. To compound matters, Adrienne and Claudette have been on a drinking binge and are absolutely no help. Sarah has been my saving grace. I don't know what I'd do without her," Mary replied, knowing love was written across her face.

"She definitely wins the wonder-child award," Jane replied.

Mary sensed Jane's creeping sadness.

"Are you and Claudette through?"

"I don't . . . know," Jane said, bursting into tears. "I feel like I'm losing my best friends and there's nothing I can do to stop it."

"I know. We'll fix it," Mary said, taking Jane in her arms.

"Please tell me how."

"Shh," Mary said, stroking Jane's head.

* * * * *

Holly poured Anne another glass of wine. They were sitting on the terrace at the Walker Art Museum.

"What are you proposing to do?" Holly asked, wiping the smudge of her fingerprint from her glass.

"About what?"

"About Jane?" Holly said, meeting her gaze.

"I don't know what you mean," Anne said, feeling furtive.

"Is this something casual? Is she still living with her wife?

"I don't know. She's been with me."

"Have you talked about it?"

Anne poured more wine, stalling. Holly was bringing her secret fears to light.

"No, we haven't talked about it."

"Doesn't that concern you? She's still involved with someone else. Someone she's been with for a long time."

Anne knew she couldn't tell Holly that Jane and Claudette had a rather open relationship, that both of them took lovers from time to time. It would send her right off the edge.

"We'll get there," Anne said.

"I just don't want you to get hurt. Jane appears to have femme fatale characteristics. I don't want you to be a casualty," Holly said.

"I know, and I appreciate you for being concerned."

"Anne, what do you want to happen?"

"I'd like to get married."

"Oh my," Holly said, pouring them both more wine.

* * * * *

Jane awoke with a start. Today was the day, and ever since she was a small girl she'd been there. How could she have forgotten? She threw on some clothes. She kissed Anne's cheek. Anne's eyes flickered open.

"Where are you going?" she asked sleepily.

"My mother's. We always plant the bulbs on this day ever since I was a kid. I almost forgot. I'll be back later. *I love you.*"

No one said *I love you* the way Jane did. Every syllable struck a chord in her soul, and Anne believed in those sounds with all of her being. The intensity of her words was as frightening as it was intoxicating. She fell back asleep with Jane's pillow wrapped up in her arms, her lover's scent still strong on the fabric.

Jane pulled up in the drive fast, remembering at the last minute that her mother was not fond of screeching tire marks on the cement. It was too late.

Hazel was already outside with her trowel, gardener's pad, and a mound of bulb sacks. She didn't look perturbed, but when she smiled her relief was evident. As a mother she'd been worried about her daughters. Fiona still wasn't answering her calls, and then Jane had gone underground as well. The knot in her stomach undid itself when Jane gave her a hug and commented on what a lovely morning it was. Jane grabbed a bag of bulbs and followed her mother to the garden.

"I thought you might have forgotten," Hazel said quietly.

"No," Jane said. "It would take something mighty

big to make me forget our family's annual event."
Falling in love had almost allowed it to slip her mind,
but love for her parents must have struck a deep
cosmic chord, deep enough to rouse her from sleep
and her lover's arms. The universe was truly an
amazing place, Jane thought, filled with cruelty,
whimsy, distress, joy, luck, and love. She felt as if
she'd experienced all of its facets this week, and she
was tired.

They planted in silence until Hazel couldn't stand
it any longer. She looked over at Jane.

"You have to tell me what's going on with you . . .
and with Fiona. I can't take another day of
wondering. I don't understand what either of you is
trying to save me from. For crissakes, I'm your
mother. Why can't you two talk to me?" Hazel
demanded.

Jane looked over at her mother, totally surprised.

"I'm sorry."

"I don't want you to be sorry. I want you to tell
me what's going on," Hazel said.

"I've fallen in love . . . perhaps for the first real
time in my life," Jane said, planting a bulb, covering
it with dirt, and wondering for a moment if love
wasn't a bit like tulips. It was in you, and then one
spring a beautiful and brilliant flower burst forth and
everyone was amazed at the miracle.

"With whom have you fallen in love?" Hazel asked
with a slightly flippant tone. She'd experienced one
too many of Jane's love affairs to take any one of
them seriously.

"Anne Beaumont," Jane replied.

"That college friend of Louise's?" Hazel inquired,
not doing a very good job at covering her surprise.

"It's not what it looks like," Jane said, instantly defensive.

"I'm sorry," Hazel said, wishing she could retract her remark. It half crossed her mind that maybe her daughters didn't confide in her because she made her judgment too quick and too apparent. Charles had been better with them in moments like these. He was the tortoise; she was the hare.

"This is real. It's not sex. It's wanting to spend a significant portion of your life with someone," Jane said, defensively.

"Okay," Hazel said, slowly.

"Why is it that you straight people have such a difficult time believing that nonstraight people can have lasting, significant relationships?" Jane declared.

"Nonstraight? Is that a new term?" Hazel asked, ever the linguist.

"Yes. You people are straight and we have about eight other titles. I put us under the umbrella term *nonstraight,*" Jane replied.

"I see."

"Do you?"

"What I see is that you have not subscribed to the usual fare, and so I have taken to judging you in those terms. If you have changed your linguistic format you should have let me know beforehand. You're in love and that's nice, but it's gotten slightly complicated, which is what, I suspect, you wish to speak about," Hazel said, reading her daughter's mind.

"Yes," Jane said, jamming a bulb rather forcefully into the freshly overturned soil.

Hazel refrained from telling her she wished she wouldn't do that. It wasn't good for the bulb.

"I don't know what to do," Jane said.

"Meaning?" Hazel said, easing back on her haunches. Getting old was not a physically comfortable situation.

"With the relationship part."

"Because you had a different kind of relationship with Claudette?" Hazel queried.

"Yes."

"Do you want to have the same kind of relationship with Anne?"

"I don't think so."

"And this concerns you?" Hazel asked.

"It's just so different..." Jane said.

"Every anarchist at some point realizes the intrinsic beauty of the system. Not necessary the system as it is practiced, but rather as it *should* be practiced."

"Is it selling out?" Jane queried. She didn't want white picket fences. All she could envision was her head impaled on one of the points.

"This is only my opinion," Hazel said cautiously, "but it seems to me that there might be something wrong with your relationship, with yourself, or with your partner that makes straying necessarily. That perhaps you're looking for something in someone other than your partner because you feel, whether rightly or wrongly, that you're missing an intrinsic ingredient."

Jane studied her mother. "Is that what happened with the Italian professor?"

Hazel swallowed hard. She hadn't told Jane that story so that it could be used as a pivotal point in a discussion on the nature of fidelity. She wasn't entirely sure why she had brought it to light after all these years. Was it the need to confess or the desire to show her daughter that even those who appear most perfect are capable of imperfection?

"I suppose so. I thought I saw in him attributes that your father did not possess. However, when I came back around I realized that I was infatuated with his desire for me and that aside from being lovers we did not make good partners."

"And good partners is better?" Jane asked, trying to keep her mind from creating a mental tally sheet of Anne's qualities versus Claudette's.

"I think so. Remember, Jane, that when you're deeply in love you do not feel the need to stray. What happened between Charles and me had more to do with me and it was a mistake, but it made me love your father more and nothing like that ever happened again. Looking back I think it was growing pains."

"Like what happened with Fiona?"

"Most likely. You see, Jane, there are people in this world who have not had a lot of lovers. So from time to time they get curious about casual liaisons, whereas you have had more than your fair share," Hazel said.

"What are you saying?" Jane asked with a quirky smile.

"That it might be time to settle down and that you probably won't suffer growing pains when you do," Hazel said.

"What scares me," Jane began slowly, "is that I thought I was deeply in love with Claudette, so it makes me wonder about the transcendental quality of love."

"How you fall out of love?" Hazel said.

"Yes. I know I must still love her because losing her is painful."

"There are different kinds of love. Perhaps what you had with Claudette was more a friendship than a relationship."

"You mean fuck buddies," Jane replied.

"You're lucky I'm not still bankrolling your allowance. That one would have cost you a significant portion," Hazel said.

They both laughed, remembering how Jane had to do twice as many chores as Fiona because she was always having to forfeit some of her allowance for her flagrant use of obscene language.

"But what I am saying is that at a certain point you and Claudette needed to make that jump into the proverbial kitchen pot and join souls. You couldn't do it, and so you shut down when you were supposed to be getting closer."

Jane nodded. She remembered the first time Claudette went home with someone else. They were at the Metro with some girls from school. An attractive older woman had taken a shine to Claudette. She turned out to be the nude model in one of Claudette's art classes. They'd spent most of the evening talking to each other. Jane had gone out to smoke a joint with some of the girls when she stumbled upon Claudette and her new friend in a compromising position. Jane didn't know what to do, so she sort of waved and then went back inside the bar and drank and danced until the bar closed.

When Claudette finally got home, Jane had pretended to be asleep. She listened as Claudette took a shower and tried not to think of another woman running her hands all over her lover. She hadn't been able to decide on a course of action. She knew that they had agreed on nonmonogamy, but Jane had naively thought that when they got a place together, having girls on the side would stop. She'd stopped taking casual lovers because living with someone and dating someone were two entirely different things. You could have more than one girlfriend when you didn't go home to one.

Claudette crawled into bed. She whispered as she pulled Jane to her, "I've been fucked all night. Now I'd like to do some fucking."

And Jane let her. She found a perverse liking in being the final desire of the evening for her lover. But she knew then she couldn't let her love get any deeper or stronger or it would kill them both. From then on Jane followed Claudette's example. When she took an interest in someone she went for it, regardless of living with Claudette or of Claudette's presence. Maybe her mother was right; maybe they were fuck buddies.

Hazel broke her train of thought. "Would you let Anne have other lovers?"

"No!"

"Why not?" Hazel asked, her blue eyes taunting.

"Because I love her too much."

Hazel handed her another bag of bulbs and they both moved over.

Jane smiled. "How come you're so smart?"

"Because I'm your mother. I'm supposed to be smart."

Jane rolled her eyes.

"Now tell me what's going on with your sister," Hazel said.

"I wish I knew. She isn't talking to me, either."

"Will you go see her?"

"Yes, I've been meaning to. Surely she's not still mad," Jane said.

"It's hard to tell with her," Hazel said, her face expressing her doubt.

"I'll go when Louise is there. Then she can't make a scene."

"Jane, that's shifty."

"Do you want me to talk to her or don't you?"

"Try and not make it obvious," Hazel warned.

Fiona heard the ping and purr of the Volkswagen as it pulled up in the drive. She wasn't angry anymore; rather, she was relieved that Jane had inadvertently been the catalyst to get her back on track. Fiona smiled warmly when she answered the door. Jane looked sheepish.

"I'm sorry."

"Me too," Fiona said, giving Jane a hug.

"I don't want to fight anymore," Jane said.

"Neither do I."

"The only reason I told Mom was because she was worried about you. I didn't want her to worry. I didn't think it was something that you'd be able to tell her. I wasn't entirely sure I could tell her," Jane said.

"You?"

"I know I'm gutsy, but wow. I was impressed."

"Impressed with what?" Louise asked, walking into the foray.

"With what Fiona is going to do with the book," Jane lied without hesitation.

Fiona let out a mental sigh. Thank god Jane was slick.

Louise gave Jane a hug, shocking everyone. "I'm glad you came by. Don't be such a stranger. I'm off. Home for dinner?"

"Yes," Fiona said.

"I'll make something special."

"Just you will be fine," Fiona teased.

"Just me?" Louise said, playing the coquette.

"I love you," Fiona said, reaching for her.

"Ditto."

"Let's have a beer on the deck," Fiona said, heading for the fridge.

"It's ten o'clock in the morning," Jane said, looking up at the clock hanging on the kitchen wall.

"It's noon somewhere. Since when has the anarchist developed a penchant for rules?"

"Since my life has become utter chaos without them," Jane replied.

"Do share," Fiona said, handing her a beer.

"Louise doesn't know, does she?" Jane said, deliberately putting the ball in Fiona's court.

"She might suspect, but it's over and we're moving on."

"Is this the first and only time?" Jane inquired.

"For me it is."

"How about her?"

"I don't know," Fiona said, beginning to feel a bit squeamish. When her life had been tidy, she craved a little dirt. Now that it had gotten dirty, she craved the soft white of innocence.

"Does that bother you?" Jane asked.

"It would have before. Now I understand how it happens. The important thing is that we're still together. That's what counts. How about you?"

"Oh my, now's there's a story. I came for some advice."

"Shoot, little sister."

"If only I had a gun."

Bel sat down on the couch in the alley. "I'm taking the two of you to AA with me if this drinking binge continues."

"Oh no, Mom's home," Adrienne said. Claudette laughed.

"I mean it. I know things are messed up right now but sitting around getting drunk all day is not going to change anything. Come have breakfast with me."

"All right, Bel," Claudette said, helping Adrienne up.

They staggered to the diner, with Bel taking charge. She got them a booth and ordered black coffees. She smiled big at the waitress, who lingered a little longer than necessary.

"What are your plans?" Bel asked, taking a sip of coffee and resuming her businesslike manner.

"Plans?" Adrienne smirked. "Let me tell you a little about plans. I started this summer with the idea of getting myself organized. I was standing on the surface of clueless then, and now I'm in the subterranean zone, an abyss without an exit."

"That was extremely poetic," Claudette said, making a mess of the ketchup.

"I never thought ketchup looked like blood," Adrienne said, slipping back to some inane childhood memory and helping Claudette get it off her sleeve.

"Girls!"

"What?" they asked, simultaneously.

"Focus, we need focus here," Bel said.

"Focus on what? The fact that we have no focus?" Claudette said.

"What if I had an idea?" Bel said.

"We could use an idea," Adrienne said, glancing over at Claudette, who looked instantly suspicious.

"You want to ship us off somewhere, don't you?" Claudette said.

"As a matter of fact..."

"I'm not going," Claudette said flatly.

"Just listen, I've got a friend in New Mexico, and she wants to get a chapter of Defenders going there. What's wrong with getting away for a little while? It would do you both good."

"We don't have a car," Claudette said.

"You could take the van. I'm not talking going forever, just a month or so. Meet some new people, see some new sights. You might like it."

"You'd let us take the van?" Adrienne said, incredulous at Bel's generosity.

"I've always considered it a company vehicle. This is a company mission," Bel said, leaning back in the booth.

Claudette and Adrienne were both silent, thinking.

"It could be fun... It's not like staying here is going to make things better," Adrienne said.

"I'll have to think about it. Let's go take a nap," Claudette said.

Bel took them back to the loft and got them settled. She tucked them in. They looked peaceful together, snuggled around each other. Funny, they didn't realize how close they'd gotten lately, Bel thought. They'd been inseparable most of the summer, and they didn't even know it. Bel wondered when they'd see it and fall into each other's arms. They'd be good for each other.

"Well?" Mary asked. "Did it work?"

"Nothing definite yet, but it will," Bel replied, sitting on the edge of Mary's desk.

"Good work, Bel."

"I don't really feel good about it. I feel kind of sneaky about our motives."

"Like whether we're being altruistic or Machiavellian?" Mary asked.

"Well, yeah," Bel said.

"It's both," Mary said decisively.

"Is that a good idea?" Bel asked, not completely convinced that she wasn't doing something bad to her friends.

"It can be, and in this case it will be because if we don't get them out of here nothing will ever get back to normal."

"I guess you're right," Bel said.

"Thank you for being the emissary."

"Speaking of relationships, how is yours going?" Bel said, raising an inquisitive eyebrow.

"Lovely, too lovely. It makes me nervous."

"Why?" Bel asked.

"Because Sarah seems too good to be true. She'll probably die of a fatal disease."

"Not a positive attitude," Bel counseled.

"Why does she like me?" Mary asked, her face riddled with confusion.

"Because you're you," Bel ventured.

"You know what I mean," Mary said.

"No, I don't," Bel said.

"She's pretty and I'm not."

"But love isn't about looks, it's about the inside stuff and darling, yours is fine."

"Thanks, Bel."

Twelve

Jane stood in the dining room, surveying the table. She straightened one of the slim white tapers that was sitting slightly off center. She wanted everything to be absolutely perfect.

"Oh shit! I'm turning into Louise," Jane said. Then she laughed, knowing no one was around and her secret was safe. She'd deny any Louise-like behavior through the most strenuous torture. I want tonight to be perfect, not because I desire to be a Martha Stewart clone. I want it to be perfect because I want Anne to remember how special she is and how much I love her, Jane told herself. That sounded like something Fiona would say. My god, we're turning into the perfect couple.

She was suddenly on the verge of having second thoughts, wavering on the precipice of doubt about her plan for the evening when she heard her mother saying, Maybe you're growing up, which is not a bad thing. It doesn't automatically mean you turn stodgy. It means you can grow into a deeper, richer person. She did feel deeper and richer, especially with regard to Anne.

It first dawned on her that she was changing when she helped Claudette move her things. They did the typical lesbian breakup thing, where one screams at the other and then both end up holding each other and crying, each trying to soothe the other's battered and torn heart. Jane suggested moving down the hall, but Claudette wouldn't have it.

"I can't handle seeing the two of you coming and going. I need some space," Claudette said.

Jane was respectful, knowing it was going to be difficult working together for a while, but they were big girls. They could do it, she assured them both. Claudette nodded, teary eyed. Jane held her. They were collecting themselves when Claudette attempted to seduce Jane. Jane wouldn't let her.

"What! You can fuck around on me, but you won't on Anne? What's the little princess have that I don't?" Claudette said, her face getting red.

Jane refrained from saying *my heart*. She has my heart, something I tried to give you but you didn't want.

"I fucked around on you because you wanted me

to. That was the deal. You didn't want to get trapped," Jane screamed back.

Now they weren't speaking. Jane didn't tell Anne about the seduction. She did tell her about the argument. She couldn't help it. She ended up crying at Anne's doorstep. Anne was patient and caring through the weeks of sodden behavior, with Jane apologizing profusely for being such a mess. Anne told her that feeling bad meant she felt things sincerely, a quality Anne held in high regard. But it didn't mean Anne didn't have her doubts.

Jane remembered the afternoon they were making love and Anne expressed her concern.

"Jane?"

"Yes," Jane said, looking up from where she was lying between Anne's legs.

"This isn't just . . . well, you know, one of your things, is it?"

"Have you been spending time with Holly?"

"Yes," Anne said, sheepishly.

"I wish there was some way I could let you inside my brain so I could show you how I feel. I feel things I never thought myself capable of, good things, different things, maybe even grown-up things. The thought of you away from me causes great psychic distress," Jane said, climbing up on Anne and feeling the length of her body. Anne wrapped her legs around Jane, pulling her closer.

Thinking back to that moment, she didn't want Anne to have the same trepidation of heart that she had felt with Claudette. It was time to jump into the pot and meld souls. She pulled the matching Goddess necklaces from her pocket. One for me, one for you, to wear forever nestled between your lovely breasts and close to your heart. Jane had convinced herself it wasn't sappy, it wasn't a mimic of the exchange of rings. It was about love and commitment. She wanted them to be committed.

The front door opened, and Anne's face lit up. "What do we have here?" she said.

Jane smiled. "The perfect romantic dinner for two."

"It looks wonderful," Anne said, giving her a hug. She looked over Jane's shoulder to the kitchen.

"And it smells wonderful too."

"That's only the beginning," Jane said.

"Of what?"

"You'll see," Jane said.

"Are you wooing me?" Anne teased.

"More than you know," Jane said, squeezing the lockets in her hand, knowing for certain she was ready.

Mary knocked her coffee over on the morning paper. She'd been up since five working on the book from the notes Fiona had given her. She hadn't read the paper yet, saving it for her break. Trying to wipe the coffee off and salvage some of the paper, she saw the article. Benton Peugh's daughter, Priscilla, was pronounced dead on arrival at Saint Joseph's after being discovered at home by her father. She had bled to death from an unspecified internal wound. Mary picked up the phone and woke Sarah.

"Good morning. Sorry to wake you."

"Never be sorry. What's up?" Sarah asked, rubbing sleep out of her eyes.

"I need you to call your friend at Mayo Clinic. Benton Peugh's daughter died last night."

"I'm sorry to hear that," Sarah said.

"I think something odd is going on. I want you to check to see if she had an illegal abortion."

"Why do you think that?"

"She bled to death."

"Oh my god."

"Exactly," Mary said, getting that queer feeling in her stomach when she sensed something bad had happened.

"Why do women do things like that?"

"Because they feel they have no other option. What would you do in her shoes?" Mary asked.

"I'll call Mayo and get back to you." Sarah avoided the question because she'd been in those shoes once.

Jane stood reading the article with Fiona doing the same over her shoulder.

"What did the nurse say?" Jane asked.

"It was a botched-up job. The police are trying to find out who performed the abortion," Mary said.

"This is awful. And Benton Peugh wonders why we want to keep it safe and legal," Jane said.

"But still this happens," Bel said, shaking her head.

"This happens because as the daughter of the country's leading antiabortion movement she did not have the option of a safe one. It would have gotten out, and she knew it would ruin her father's career," Mary replied.

"That's love for you," Sarah said sadly.

"Where are Adrienne and Claudette? We need them here," Jane said.

"Do you think that's a good idea?" Mary asked.

"This isn't about who is sleeping with whom. This is work," Jane said firmly.

"We aren't going to make a media circus out of this, are we?" Mary asked nervously.

"No, but we are going to show our respects," Jane replied.

"We're going to the funeral?" Sarah asked, instantly mortified.

"Yes. As women we mourn her needless death; as activists we implore others never to let this happen again; as human beings we help a father bury his only child," Jane said.

Fiona wrote that down. It would be the preface to the book. She looked at her sister, smiling in admiration.

"You're beautiful, Jane," Fiona said, giving her a hug.

"In your eyes . . ." Jane replied.

"You can't always help falling in and out of love. You told me that once. It was good advice," Fiona said.

"I know. I love Anne. I can't deny that, but Claudette . . . it hurts. I've never hurt like this, or felt like this," Jane said.

"It'll get better."

"Will it?"

"After it stops haunting you," Fiona replied, thinking she still thought about Adrienne every day, still craved things she could no longer have. You never just walk away, she thought. Whoever said that lied.

Claudette and Adrienne drank several cups of coffee and tried with great difficulty to remain collected while Jane outlined the plan. It was simple. The Defenders would dress appropriately, act with deference, and show their respects in a calm, quiet manner. They all felt out of character.

"I know it's hard, but it would really be bad press to fuck up a funeral. We'll hang light, but the battle continues when he's had a chance to recover," Jane said.

"Do you think he will be able to recover from this?" Sarah asked.

"I don't know. What do you do when your own nemesis slaps you in the face?" Jane said.

"Run," Adrienne said, looking deeply at Fiona and knowing this would be the last time she'd see her. She wasn't coming back. She knew already.

It was raining the day of the funeral. Just like in the movies, Jane thought. She looked over at Claudette, feeling pain in the place where her love had once lived. How to say good-bye? Claudette walked toward her while the priest read the benediction. She took Jane's hand and squeezed.

"I have known you longer than anyone in my life. I know this is hard and I will always love you, but it's time. Okay?" Claudette whispered.

Jane nodded, feeling tears run down her face. She put her umbrella down and let the rain douse her. When the sermon was over, Jane walked to the casket and laid a single white lily on top. She looked over at Benton Peugh and took his hand.

A few of the publications of
THE NAIAD PRESS, INC.
P.O. Box 10543   Tallahassee, Florida 32302
Phone (850) 539-5965
Toll-Free Order Number: 1-800-533-1973
Web Site: WWW.NAIADPRESS.COM
Mail orders welcome. Please include 15% postage.
Write or call for our free catalog which also features an
incredible selection of lesbian videos.

THE DRIVE by Trisha Todd. 176 pp. The star of *Claire of the Moon* tells all!   ISBN 1-56280-237-2 $11.95

BOTH SIDES by Saxon Bennett. 240 pp. A community of women falling in and out of love.   ISBN 1-56280-236-4   11.95

WATERMARK by Karin Kallmaker. 256 pp. One burning question . . . how to lead her back to love?   ISBN 1-56280-235-6   11.95

THE OTHER WOMAN by Ann O'Leary. 240 pp. Her roguish way draws women like a magnet.   ISBN 1-56280-234-8   11.95

SILVER THREADS by Lyn Denison.208 pp. Finding her way back to love . . .   ISBN 1-56280-231-3   11.95

CHIMNEY ROCK BLUES by Janet McClellan. 224 pp. 4th Tru North mystery.   ISBN 1-56280-233-X   11.95

OMAHA'S BELL by Penny Hayes. 208 pp. Orphaned Keeley Delaney woos the lovely Prudence Morris.   ISBN 1-56280-232-1   11.95

SIXTH SENSE by Kate Calloway. 224 pp. 6th Cassidy James mystery.   ISBN 1-56280-228-3   11.95

DAWN OF THE DANCE by Marianne K. Martin. 224 pp. A dance with an old friend, nothing more . . . yeah!   ISBN 1-56280-229-1   11.95

WEDDING BELL BLUES by Julia Watts. 240 pp. Love, family, and a recipe for success.   ISBN 1-56280-230-5   11.95

THOSE WHO WAIT by Peggy J. Herring. 160 pp. Two sisters . . . in love with the same woman.   ISBN 1-56280-223-2   11.95

WHISPERS IN THE WIND by Frankie J. Jones. 192 pp. "If you don't want this," she whispered, "all you have to say is 'stop.' "   ISBN 1-56280-226-7   11.95

WHEN SOME BODY DISAPPEARS by Therese Szymanski. 192 pp. 3rd Brett Higgins mystery.   ISBN 1-56280-227-5   11.95

THE WAY LIFE SHOULD BE by Diana Braund. 240 pp. Which one will teach her the true meaning of love?   ISBN 1-56280-221-6   11.95

UNTIL THE END by Kaye Davis. 256pp. 3rd Maris Middleton
mystery.   ISBN 1-56280-222-4   11.95

FIFTH WHEEL by Kate Calloway. 224 pp. 5th Cassidy James
mystery.   ISBN 1-56280-218-6   11.95

JUST YESTERDAY by Linda Hill. 176 pp. Reliving all the
passion of yesterday.   ISBN 1-56280-219-4   11.95

THE TOUCH OF YOUR HAND edited by Barbara Grier and
Christine Cassidy. 304 pp. Erotic love stories by Naiad Press
authors.   ISBN 1-56280-220-8   14.95

WINDROW GARDEN by Janet McClellan. 192 pp. They discover
a passion they never dreamed possible.   ISBN 1-56280-216-X   11.95

PAST DUE by Claire McNab. 224 pp. 10th Carol Ashton
mystery.   ISBN 1-56280-217-8   11.95

CHRISTABEL by Laura Adams. 224 pp. Two captive hearts and
the passion that will set them free.   ISBN 1-56280-214-3   11.95

PRIVATE PASSIONS by Laura DeHart Young. 192 pp. An
unforgettable new portrait of lesbian love . . .   ISBN 1-56280-215-1   11.95

BAD MOON RISING by Barbara Johnson. 208 pp. 2nd Colleen
Fitzgerald mystery.   ISBN 1-56280-211-9   11.95

RIVER QUAY by Janet McClellan. 208 pp. 3rd Tru North
mystery.   ISBN 1-56280-212-7   11.95

ENDLESS LOVE by Lisa Shapiro. 272 pp. To believe, once
again, that love can be forever.   ISBN 1-56280-213-5   11.95

FALLEN FROM GRACE by Pat Welch. 256 pp. 6th Helen Black
mystery.   ISBN 1-56280-209-7   11.95

THE NAKED EYE by Catherine Ennis. 208 pp. Her lover in the
camera's eye . . .   ISBN 1-56280-210-0   11.95

OVER THE LINE by Tracey Richardson. 176 pp. 2nd Stevie
Houston mystery.   ISBN 1-56280-202-X   11.95

JULIA'S SONG by Ann O'Leary. 208 pp. Strangely
disturbing . . . strangely exciting.   ISBN 1-56280-197-X   11.95

LOVE IN THE BALANCE by Marianne K. Martin. 256 pp.
Weighing the costs of love . . .   ISBN 1-56280-199-6   11.95

PIECE OF MY HEART by Julia Watts. 208 pp. All the
stuff that dreams are made of —   ISBN 1-56280-206-2   11.95

MAKING UP FOR LOST TIME by Karin Kallmaker. 240 pp.
Nobody does it better . . .   ISBN 1-56280-196-1   11.95

GOLD FEVER by Lyn Denison. 224 pp. By author of *Dream
Lover*.   ISBN 1-56280-201-1   11.95

WHEN THE DEAD SPEAK by Therese Szymanski. 224 pp. 2nd
Brett Higgins mystery.   ISBN 1-56280-198-8   11.95

FOURTH DOWN by Kate Calloway. 240 pp. 4th Cassidy James
mystery.   ISBN 1-56280-205-4   11.95

A MOMENT'S INDISCRETION by Peggy J. Herring. 176 pp.
There's a fine line between love and lust . . .   ISBN 1-56280-194-5   11.95

CITY LIGHTS/COUNTRY CANDLES by Penny Hayes. 208 pp.
About the women she has known . . .   ISBN 1-56280-195-3   11.95

POSSESSIONS by Kaye Davis. 240 pp. 2nd Maris Middleton
mystery.   ISBN 1-56280-192-9   11.95

A QUESTION OF LOVE by Saxon Bennett. 208 pp. Every
woman is granted one great love.   ISBN 1-56280-205-4   11.95

RHYTHM TIDE by Frankie J. Jones. 160 pp.   . . . to desire
passionately and be passionately desired.   ISBN 1-56280-189-9   11.95

PENN VALLEY PHOENIX by Janet McClellan. 208 pp. 2nd
Tru North Mystery.   ISBN 1-56280-200-3   11.95

BY RESERVATION ONLY by Jackie Calhoun. 240 pp. A
chance for true happiness.   ISBN 1-56280-191-0   11.95

OLD BLACK MAGIC by Jaye Maiman. 272 pp. 9th Robin
Miller mystery.   ISBN 1-56280-175-9   11.95

LEGACY OF LOVE by Marianne K. Martin. 240 pp. Women
will do anything for her . . .   ISBN 1-56280-184-8   11.95

LETTING GO by Ann O'Leary. 160 pp. Laura, at 39, in love
with 23-year-old Kate.   ISBN 1-56280-183-X   11.95

LADY BE GOOD edited by Barbara Grier and Christine Cassidy.
288 pp. Erotic stories by Naiad Press authors.   ISBN 1-56280-180-5   14.95

CHAIN LETTER by Claire McNab. 288 pp. 9th Carol Ashton
mystery.   ISBN 1-56280-181-3   11.95

NIGHT VISION by Laura Adams. 256 pp. Erotic fantasy romance
by "famous" author.   ISBN 1-56280-182-1   11.95

SEA TO SHINING SEA by Lisa Shapiro. 256 pp. Unable to resist
the raging passion . . .   ISBN 1-56280-177-5   11.95

THIRD DEGREE by Kate Calloway. 224 pp. 3rd Cassidy James
mystery.   ISBN 1-56280-185-6   11.95

WHEN THE DANCING STOPS by Therese Szymanski. 272 pp.
1st Brett Higgins mystery.   ISBN 1-56280-186-4   11.95

PHASES OF THE MOON by Julia Watts. 192 pp. . . . . . hungry
for everything life has to offer.   ISBN 1-56280-176-7   11.95

BABY IT'S COLD by Jaye Maiman. 256 pp. 5th Robin Miller
mystery.   ISBN 1-56280-156-2   10.95

CLASS REUNION by Linda Hill. 176 pp. The girl from her
past . . .   ISBN 1-56280-178-3   11.95

DREAM LOVER by Lyn Denison. 224 pp. A soft, sensuous,
romantic fantasy.   ISBN 1-56280-173-1   11.95

FORTY LOVE by Diana Simmonds. 288 pp. Joyous, heart-
warming romance.   ISBN 1-56280-171-6   11.95

IN THE MOOD by Robbi Sommers. 160 pp. The queen of
erotic tension!   ISBN 1-56280-172-4   11.95

SWIMMING CAT COVE by Lauren Douglas. 192 pp. 2nd
Allison O'Neil Mystery.   ISBN 1-56280-168-6   11.95

THE LOVING LESBIAN by Claire McNab and Sharon Gedan.
240 pp. Explore the experiences that make lesbian love unique.
           ISBN 1-56280-169-4   14.95

COURTED by Celia Cohen. 160 pp. Sparkling romantic
encounter.   ISBN 1-56280-166-X   11.95

SEASONS OF THE HEART by Jackie Calhoun. 240 pp. Romance
through the years.   ISBN 1-56280-167-8   11.95

K. C. BOMBER by Janet McClellan. 208 pp. 1st Tru North
mystery.   ISBN 1-56280-157-0   11.95

LAST RITES by Tracey Richardson. 192 pp. 1st Stevie Houston
mystery.   ISBN 1-56280-164-3   11.95

EMBRACE IN MOTION by Karin Kallmaker. 256 pp. A whirlwind
love affair.   ISBN 1-56280-165-1   11.95

HOT CHECK by Peggy J. Herring. 192 pp. Will workaholic Alice
fall for guitarist Ricky?   ISBN 1-56280-163-5   11.95

OLD TIES by Saxon Bennett. 176 pp. Can Cleo surrender to a
passionate new love?   ISBN 1-56280-159-7   11.95

LOVE ON THE LINE by Laura DeHart Young. 176 pp. Will Stef
win Kay's heart?   ISBN 1-56280-162-7   11.95

DEVIL'S LEG CROSSING by Kaye Davis. 192 pp. 1st Maris
Middleton mystery.   ISBN 1-56280-158-9   11.95

COSTA BRAVA by Marta Balletbo Coll. 144 pp. Read the book,
see the movie!   ISBN 1-56280-153-8   11.95

MEETING MAGDALENE & OTHER STORIES by
Marilyn Freeman. 144 pp. Read the book, see the movie!
           ISBN 1-56280-170-8   11.95

SECOND FIDDLE by Kate 208 pp. 2nd P.I. Cassidy James
mystery.   ISBN 1-56280-169-6   11.95

LAUREL by Isabel Miller. 128 pp. By the author of the beloved
Patience and Sarah.   ISBN 1-56280-146-5   10.95

LOVE OR MONEY by Jackie Calhoun. 240 pp. The romance of
real life.   ISBN 1-56280-147-3   10.95

SMOKE AND MIRRORS by Pat Welch. 224 pp. 5th Helen Black
Mystery.   ISBN 1-56280-143-0   10.95

DANCING IN THE DARK edited by Barbara Grier & Christine Cassidy. 272 pp. Erotic love stories by Naiad Press authors.
ISBN 1-56280-144-9   14.95

TIME AND TIME AGAIN by Catherine Ennis. 176 pp. Passionate love affair.   ISBN 1-56280-145-7   10.95

PAXTON COURT by Diane Salvatore. 256 pp. Erotic and wickedly funny contemporary tale about the business of learning to live together.   ISBN 1-56280-114-7   10.95

INNER CIRCLE by Claire McNab. 208 pp. 8th Carol Ashton Mystery.   ISBN 1-56280-135-X   11.95

LESBIAN SEX: AN ORAL HISTORY by Susan Johnson. 240 pp. Need we say more?   ISBN 1-56280-142-2   14.95

WILD THINGS by Karin Kallmaker. 240 pp. By the undisputed mistress of lesbian romance.   ISBN 1-56280-139-2   11.95

THE GIRL NEXT DOOR by Mindy Kaplan. 208 pp. Just what you d expect.   ISBN 1-56280-140-6   11.95

NOW AND THEN by Penny Hayes. 240 pp. Romance on the westward journey.   ISBN 1-56280-121-X   11.95

HEART ON FIRE by Diana Simmonds. 176 pp. The romantic and erotic rival of *Curious Wine*.   ISBN 1-56280-152-X   11.95

DEATH AT LAVENDER BAY by Lauren Wright Douglas. 208 pp. 1st Allison O'Neil Mystery.   ISBN 1-56280-085-X   11.95

YES I SAID YES I WILL by Judith McDaniel. 272 pp. Hot romance by famous author.   ISBN 1-56280-138-4   11.95

FORBIDDEN FIRES by Margaret C. Anderson. Edited by Mathilda Hills. 176 pp. Famous author's "unpublished" Lesbian romance.
ISBN 1-56280-123-6   21.95

SIDE TRACKS by Teresa Stores. 160 pp. Gender-bending Lesbians on the road.   ISBN 1-56280-122-8   10.95

WILDWOOD FLOWERS by Julia Watts. 208 pp. Hilarious and heart-warming tale of true love.   ISBN 1-56280-127-9   10.95

NEVER SAY NEVER by Linda Hill. 224 pp. Rule #1: Never get involved with . . .   ISBN 1-56280-126-0   11.95

THE WISH LIST by Saxon Bennett. 192 pp. Romance through the years.   ISBN 1-56280-125-2   10.95

OUT OF THE NIGHT by Kris Bruyer. 192 pp. Spine-tingling thriller.   ISBN 1-56280-120-1   10.95

LOVE'S HARVEST by Peggy J. Herring. 176 pp. by the author of *Once More With Feeling*.   ISBN 1-56280-117-1   10.95

FAMILY SECRETS by Laura DeHart Young. 208 pp. Enthralling romance and suspense.   ISBN 1-56280-119-8   10.95

INLAND PASSAGE by Jane Rule. 288 pp. Tales exploring conventional & unconventional relationships.   ISBN 0-930044-56-8   10.95

DOUBLE BLUFF by Claire McNab. 208 pp. 7th Carol Ashton Mystery.   ISBN 1-56280-096-5   10.95

BAR GIRLS by Lauran Hoffman. 176 pp. See the movie, read the book!   ISBN 1-56280-115-5   10.95

THE FIRST TIME EVER edited by Barbara Grier & Christine Cassidy. 272 pp. Love stories by Naiad Press authors.   ISBN 1-56280-086-8   14.95

MISS PETTIBONE AND MISS McGRAW by Brenda Weathers. 208 pp. A charming ghostly love story.   ISBN 1-56280-151-1   10.95

CHANGES by Jackie Calhoun. 208 pp. Involved romance and relationships.   ISBN 1-56280-083-3   10.95

FAIR PLAY by Rose Beecham. 256 pp. An Amanda Valentine Mystery.   ISBN 1-56280-081-7   10.95

PAYBACK by Celia Cohen. 176 pp. A gripping thriller of romance, revenge and betrayal.   ISBN 1-56280-084-1   10.95

THE BEACH AFFAIR by Barbara Johnson. 224 pp. Sizzling summer romance/mystery/intrigue.   ISBN·1-56280-090-6   10.95

GETTING THERE by Robbi Sommers. 192 pp. Nobody does it like Robbi!   ISBN 1-56280-099-X   10.95

FINAL CUT by Lisa Haddock. 208 pp. 2nd Carmen Ramirez Mystery.   ISBN 1-56280-088-4   10.95

FLASHPOINT by Katherine V. Forrest. 256 pp. A Lesbian blockbuster!   ISBN 1-56280-079-5   10.95

CLAIRE OF THE MOON by Nicole Conn. Audio Book — Read by Marianne Hyatt.   ISBN 1-56280-113-9   16.95

FOR LOVE AND FOR LIFE: INTIMATE PORTRAITS OF LESBIAN COUPLES by Susan Johnson. 224 pp.   ISBN 1-56280-091-4   14.95

DEVOTION by Mindy Kaplan. 192 pp. See the movie — read the book!   ISBN 1-56280-093-0   10.95

SOMEONE TO WATCH by Jaye Maiman. 272 pp. 4th Robin Miller Mystery.   ISBN 1-56280-095-7   10.95

GREENER THAN GRASS by Jennifer Fulton. 208 pp. A young woman — a stranger in her bed.   ISBN 1-56280-092-2   10.95

TRAVELS WITH DIANA HUNTER by Regine Sands. Erotic lesbian romp. Audio Book (2 cassettes)   ISBN 1-56280-107-4   16.95

CABIN FEVER by Carol Schmidt. 256 pp. Sizzling suspense and passion.   ISBN 1-56280-089-1   10.95

THERE WILL BE NO GOODBYES by Laura DeHart Young. 192 pp. Romantic love, strength, and friendship.   ISBN 1-56280-103-1   10.95

FAULTLINE by Sheila Ortiz Taylor. 144 pp. Joyous comic
lesbian novel.   ISBN 1-56280-108-2   9.95

OPEN HOUSE by Pat Welch. 176 pp. 4th Helen Black Mystery.
                                                      ISBN 1-56280-102-3   10.95

ONCE MORE WITH FEELING by Peggy J. Herring. 240 pp.
Lighthearted, loving romantic adventure.   ISBN 1-56280-089-2   11.95

WHISPERS by Kris Bruyer. 176 pp. Romantic ghost story.
                                                      ISBN 1-56280-082-5   10.95

NIGHT SONGS by Penny Mickelbury. 224 pp. 2nd Gianna
Maglione Mystery.   ISBN 1-56280-097-3   10.95

GETTING TO THE POINT by Teresa Stores. 256 pp. Classic
southern Lesbian novel.   ISBN 1-56280-100-7   10.95

PAINTED MOON by Karin Kallmaker. 224 pp. Delicious
Kallmaker romance.   ISBN 1-56280-075-2   11.95

THE MYSTERIOUS NAIAD edited by Katherine V. Forrest &
Barbara Grier. 320 pp. Love stories by Naiad Press authors.
                                                      ISBN 1-56280-074-4   14.95

DAUGHTERS OF A CORAL DAWN by Katherine V. Forrest.
240 pp. Tenth Anniversay Edition.   ISBN 1-56280-104-X   11.95

BODY GUARD by Claire McNab. 208 pp. 6th Carol Ashton
Mystery.   ISBN 1-56280-073-6   11.95

CACTUS LOVE by Lee Lynch. 192 pp. Stories by the beloved
storyteller.   ISBN 1-56280-071-X   9.95

SECOND GUESS by Rose Beecham. 216 pp. An Amanda
Valentine Mystery.   ISBN 1-56280-069-8   9.95

A RAGE OF MAIDENS by Lauren Wright Douglas. 240 pp.
6th Caitlin Reece Mystery.   ISBN 1-56280-068-X   10.95

TRIPLE EXPOSURE by Jackie Calhoun. 224 pp. Romantic
drama involving many characters.   ISBN 1-56280-067-1   10.95

PERSONAL ADS by Robbi Sommers. 176 pp. Sizzling short
stories.   ISBN 1-56280-059-0   11.95

CROSSWORDS by Penny Sumner. 256 pp. 2nd Victoria Cross
Mystery.   ISBN 1-56280-064-7   9.95

SWEET CHERRY WINE by Carol Schmidt. 224 pp. A novel of
suspense.   ISBN 1-56280-063-9   9.95

These are just a few of the many Naiad Press titles — we are the oldest and
largest lesbian/feminist publishing company in the world. We also offer an
enormous selection of lesbian video products. Please request a complete
catalog. We offer personal service; we encourage and welcome direct mail
orders from individuals who have limited access to bookstores carrying our
publications.

LOOKING FOR NAIAD?

Buy our books at
www.naiadpress.com

or call our toll-free number
1-800-533-1973

or by fax (24 hours a day)
1-850-539-9731